**Dedicated to my n
Alex a**

"[1]The most beautif
those who have kno
known struggle, kno .... have found their
way out of the depths. These persons have an
appreciation, a sensitivity, and an understanding of
life that fills them with compassion, gentleness,
and a deep loving concern. Beautiful people do
not just happen."

Elisabeth Kübler-Ross

"[2]Religion is for people who are afraid of going to
hell, Spirituality is for people who've been there".

Vine Deloria Jr

Acknowledgements

I would like to thank those people who were so positive about the idea of me writing a book in the first place namely; Uncle Norman, Jay, Douglas, Frances, Maureen and mediums; Suzanne and Louise.

Everyone who gave me valuable critical feedback; Adianna, Amelia, Anna, Celia, Clare, Gabrielle, Greg, Jane, Lindsay, Pat, Pauline, Rachel, Ross, Shirley and Valia.

Tom who got me moving again when I was stuck.

Maggi, who helped enormously with proof reading and who has always reminded me of my strengths, as a boss and a friend.

With very special thanks to Dave, who responded so well to my first few pages. For his editorial input, and encouraging me to keep going until the very end.

Front cover from original artwork by Author

For Lake who barely knew her Dad

Introduction

Over the last 35 years I have read a large variety of books relating to the life of mediums, psychic phenomena, life after death and other related matters. When I begin to read a new book I often sigh when I read the psychic credentials of the author who has usually had amazing experiences of the spirit world from a young age, seeing spirits and talking to invisible friends. They often have a guiding grandmother who is also sensitive to this world. I mean no disrespect but I can't relate to that as that has not been my experience. Heaven is available to all of us, messages from there are often subtle and easily dismissed, but if we give more attention to signs around us, especially at difficult times in our life, there is a lot to be gained.

I'm not trying to prove anything to anyone, but I know a lot of people are frightened of dying or are stuck in grief wondering where the people and animals they love have gone when they die. I hope this book can bring a ray of hope.

I have included recipes from my mother's cookbook from over 50 years ago. Recipes are like spells; they have a power to connect you to the past, allowing the magic to pour back through time into the dish. I also believe emotions can be stirred into dishes when they are created and those feelings transferred to the guests when they eat them, so be mindful of your emotions when you are cooking!

Prologue

We fling open the car doors and race with our beach bags towards the golden sand. Shelley's parents gather the picnic and lock the car. The beach is fairly empty, just a few local French lads kicking a ball about and showing off to a group of girls.

Entering the surf brings blessed relief from the heat of the car. Soon all four of us are enjoying the huge Atlantic waves. There's a slight breeze which ruffles the red flag posted nearby in the sand. It's a clear, sunny day and we can see for miles around.

Cameron playfully splashes his wife with water, teasing her to get her hair wet. Aileen is laughing so much she loses her balance when the next wave comes crashing down, soaking her completely.

"You're like a couple of teenagers", their daughter Shelley exclaims.

I ride the waves, flying towards the shore like a surfer. It's been great spending time with Shelley and her family. They always have a good time and know how to enjoy themselves. After about 20 minutes Shelley's mother, Aileen, suggests we go in and have something to eat, and heads towards the shore. Shelley starts to follow her, leaving Cameron and me enjoying the waves a bit longer.

I start swimming in. Cameron is about 20 feet away from me and is doing the same. The waves actually carry us forward with quite a surge which helps. I'm looking forward to the picnic as I'm starting to feel really hungry after all the activity. Aileen is on the sand now and Shelley is about 20 feet from her mother. I look ahead of me and realise I am no further in. In fact, after the wave has pulled me rushing in, it pulls me back out.

I look around at the horizon and notice we have drifted quite a distance from the shore and the swell seems to be picking up strength. I glance over to Cameron and feel a sense of danger flash through me as I notice he is struggling too. I swim harder but the waves keep submerging me and I'm starting to tire. I shout to my school friend,

"Shelley, I can't get in!"
Her mother, Aileen is taking it all in. She's a calm and sensible woman but she is showing signs of anguish at our predicament which is becoming increasingly treacherous.
"You can get in Rose, you can!" her mother screams.

I'm now ducking under the water for longer periods of time, and try as I might I can't make any headway. Great gulps of seawater are adding to my fear. Cameron is waving frantically and Aileen, is concerned that he might be having an asthma attack. She starts shouting at the young men on the beach to help him; one of them moves towards the surf.

I'm so exhausted it gradually dawns on me that my efforts are futile. I continue to struggle but my strength is diminishing, I am literally out of my depth. My fatigue is overwhelming despite my rising panic and adrenaline.   Gradually......... and reluctantly........... I submit to the power of the ocean. I give up hope, and in that same moment a strange calm descends over me as .... I disappear under the dark, green water for the last time..................

Early Days

The creamy, orange gunge was being shovelled into my mouth at such a rate my breathing couldn't keep up. Fortunately my mother would occasionally leave the room and allow me to catch my breath. I tried to explain with my eyes and hands that I was being fed too quickly, but without the facility of language it was impossible.

This is my earliest memory. I'm marooned in a high chair in the centre of a large kitchen in East Finchley, North London, and my mother is feeding me lunch. Despite the fear of not being able to breathe and not being equipped to communicate this, it stands as a comforting memory, indicating a time when I secured a large chunk of my mother's attention in lieu of my older, and less dependent siblings.

My name is Rose, I am the youngest of four, two boys and two girls. Despite having an excellent memory I sadly don't recall my father being around much when I was very young. I have one memory as a baby of an explosive argument taking place above my head, which seemed to have something to do with the washing machine, my mother ending up in tears.

It's funny how inanimate objects can become the catalyst for expressing pent up feelings of intense heartache. It was as if by opening the door of the washing machine, anger and retribution could more easily pour out alongside the colourful clothes that represented far sweeter moments in the

couple's past. My Dad was seeing another woman
and my mother knew. It must have broken her
heart. They had married young and very much in
love. He never fell out of love with her but
claimed instead it was possible to be in love with
two people at the same time. Suffice to say, after a
long period of emotional difficulty, my parents'
marriage ended due to the third person invited in
by my father. He left the family home but would
turn up to take me and my siblings out to a park or
somewhere he could spend some time with us.

***

There's a knock at the door; my mother walks
through the house to let him in.
    "Your Dad's here!" she announces. We are
gathered in the living room, sitting pensively
clasping our bags. She runs her hands through her
bleached, blonde bob, her dress is a pretty paisley
print in black and orange. "They need to be back
by 5 pm" she states. "They've got packed lunches
and fruit. Make sure Rose doesn't get too cold".
    My Dad is wearing cream trousers and a
pale blue short-sleeved shirt and sporting mirrored
sunglasses. They are a good looking couple.
    We pile into his cream Triumph Dolomite
and set off to the swimming pool. On arrival our
Dad pays us in and leads us to a space on the grass
near the pool to lay our blanket and leave our stuff.
It's an outdoor pool and the weather is warm and
sunny. My brothers Robert and Alex get changed
and run off to the water. My sister Ruth and I

already have our costumes on but are helped out of our clothes by Dad. When my brothers return, Dad takes Ruth and me over to the pool as neither of us can swim at the age of 5 and 4 years respectively. Ruth makes a beeline for the turquoise chute jutting into the sparkling water. Instinctively I tag behind. Dad gets in the water to catch us. Ruth climbs the steps, pauses for a few seconds then slides down into her father's arms. I am left deliberating at the top whilst my Dad tries to persuade me to follow suit.

"Just sit down with your legs straight and I will catch you", he coaxed.

"I can't" I responded despite the pressure of the queue that was building behind me.

"It's perfectly safe", he offers.

I had a built-in radar for danger and wasn't convinced. Perhaps if he hadn't broken my mother's trust he might not have broken mine, it was too much to ask. He might get distracted and forget to catch me. After what seemed like ages the impatient queue begrudgingly retreats, and releases me from my public ordeal.

***

Down the road from where we lived were very close friends of my mother's called Liz and James Findley. They were a Scottish couple and maybe that cemented their friendship, as my mother had been evacuated to Scotland during the war so there was familiarity there. Liz and my mother met at the local church. They discovered much common ground and an unspoken understanding of the challenges of raising children. Liz had two sons and a daughter. The couple became lifelong friends. After my father was asked to leave, my mother took action to increase her financial income. Ever-present Liz and James helped to decorate the rooms and make them rent-worthy in record time, and my mother secured some paying lodgers. She also took in foster children for short and long term care.

Now that my mother was on her own, the Findleys were drafted in to help with an emergency. Alex was a fearless, adventurous little boy and James kindly replaced the glass door a couple of times after Alex had gone through it, miraculously unharmed. They would baby-sit when my mother had an important appointment to attend with the solicitor regarding the divorce or such like. It's comforting to know my mother had such good support during those difficult days.

The lodgers were a kind couple from Ghana called Jimmy and Carmel. They had the room upstairs at the back of the house, and they kept green parrots in their room which they let us feed with sunflower seeds. Donna was a foster child who came to us aged about two; her family were also from Ghana. We all adored her, though at first I felt threatened when I was no longer the youngest member of the family, to be bathed and fed first. Donna had a grandmother called Mrs Nee Owoo, who sometimes stayed. She was small, round and a bit scary. She wore bold and colourful clothes with a headscarf. As a treat she would make homemade banana fritters, which she sizzled in hot butter and sprinkled with nutmeg and sugar before dishing out. Her cooking aromas clung to her like culinary perfume.

A number of children were fostered with us but Donna stayed the longest. I remember David, who fell asleep in his dinner and a child whose name was so difficult to pronounce he was affectionately referred to as "the other one". Liz was accompanying my mother to the shops one time and was outside keeping an eye on the pram. It was one of those enormous old prams that could fit two youngsters in. A lady approached to coo over what she presumed were twins, but on seeing a white and a black baby was completely lost for words. It was the late 1960's but this was a step too far.

Once the divorce was underway my mother made the courageous decision to move back North, to her hometown, Newcastle upon Tyne, the equivalent, in a game of chess, of taking out the queen and suggesting he put it where the sun don't shine. A brave move, however with four children in tow, aged 5 -12 years, it can't have been easy. The month before, Liz had broken the difficult news to her that they would be returning to Scotland for James's work. It was a devastating blow and would have made it untenable for my mother to stay in London on her own,

'She was being held together by sellotape', I heard Liz say; however the link to the Findleys would never be broken.

At the age of 5 years old, I said goodbye to

my school friends with a mixture of sadness and excitement. We headed North with Jane the cat and our Cockney accents onboard to begin a new chapter.

My Shire[3]

The day we moved in to our new home in Newcastle the sun endlessly shone. We watched our furniture being carried down the long ramp from the back of a huge removal van. Our hall seat, crafted with swirls on its dark, wood body; the bureau, where important papers were kept, along with our christening napkin rings and other treasured items; tea chests filled with books, clothes and other belongings. If we were quick my sister and I could run up and down the ramp before the men came back out for more stuff.

We heard strange accents around us but amazingly my mother could understand them. There was much to explore. I felt safe with my mother and siblings around me. In the absence of a father, Alex and Robert became the protectors of the pack.

"Why don't you all go and investigate the shops along the road?"
my mother suggested whilst dishing out coins to us. "Get a pint of milk and some biscuits?" she directed to Robert the oldest, "and watch the roads!"

I returned from our first visit to the corner store having spent my 10p on ten Bubbly's. I noted with surprise my mother's lack of objection but I suppose she had more important things on her mind.

At the top of our street was a moor, known locally as the 'Little Moor'. Popular with dog walkers, the winding grey paths were smooth and long, so became the best place for my sister and I to roller skate. At the bottom was the 'Valley', a large green dip, the main place to hang out. Next to it a storm drain known as the 'Sewer' and a good place to explore and make dens. Here grew an area of dense foliage with a steep bank up the side so you were invisible from the road. The 'Big Tree' was fastened with a rope swing that swung high, up over the stream below.

The stream was a source of great activity; hours were spent building dams to redirect the water to create pools and waterfalls. In a fairly short time our new home became our 'Shire'. It's hard to imagine children today getting pleasure from such simple and free activities, and incidentally no one ever got their eye taken out.

Long summer days in the 1970's were spent on the 'Valley'. Local kids of all ages were drawn in to play, like cold hands to a fire. Rounders was the biggest pull, even the local hard knocks joined in. The sun browned our skin whilst the sweet aroma of freshly cut grass hung in the air along with the odd cloud of midges. There weren't any mobiles to wind us in on invisible cords; parents trusted we would come back safe and hopefully tired. We knew to head home for tea around 5 pm, and in the summer it was straight back out until the sun went down.

Homemade clubs with secret passwords came and went. Ruth and I were allowed to join Alex's gang, where you were presented with an enormously important coin-shaped ring. Alex was a natural leader and effortlessly attracted an entourage of adoring females and males alike. He followed his own drum beat, his shoulder-length, fair hair and blue eyes adding to his allure. He'd ask me to nip to the corner shop for him to get a large bag of Minstrels and a two-pack of Mr Kipling apple pies, which he would eat in his room stretched out on his bed. He rewarded me with the change but as one of his biggest fans I would have obliged without payment.

My eldest brother Robert was a more insular fellow. He studied hard, sometimes taking his desk outside in the yard to revise whilst enjoying the sun on his stripped off back. He spent many hours in his room putting together airfix planes and decorating them from tiny tins of airfix paints with specific names; Sunset Red, Duck Egg Blue and Dark Admiral Grey. It wasn't all study and no play though. Robert had a fantastic laugh and wasn't afraid to use it. He had a real passion and sensitivity for creatures and often nursed an injured bird, which he safely hid in the dining room away from our cat Jane. He would have made a fantastic vet, administering to animals whilst lifting the spirits of their worried owners with his infectious optimism. Robert collected skulls and bones from our long country walks on holidays in Northumberland. They were displayed on his shelves like museum specimens below planes suspended from the ceiling by fishing wire. It was quite an experience visiting Robert in his room.

My sister Ruth and I had 15 months between us so we had shared everything from bedroom to bath time. Typically we were often bought the same present or clothing. Ruth would choose the blue or green one and I'd opt for red or brown, or at a push, purple. At our mother's strong suggestion, our Dad bought us both a bike for Christmas. We had never had one before and used to borrow from our friends. Mine was purple and Ruth's was green, and they folded up so they could stay in the hallway for easy access. We spent many summers cycling around the neighbourhood, between favourite parks and discovering new ones, carrying supplies of pop, crisps and sweets. Occasionally we'd meet hostility from youths if we were outside of our area, but we had each other's back and were both prepared to fight. We were carefree and cared for, everyone knew each other's families around the streets, and there was a real sense of community.

Our cousins from Yorkshire and Cheshire would visit a few times a year, but usually in the summer, around Christmas or at Easter. I adored creating treasure hunts for my sister but especially for cousin Mark as he was younger than me and more easily impressed. Paper clues with riddles and drawings directed him to specific objects around our house or in the outside vicinity. I even persuaded the local shopkeeper to take part when Mark was directed to the local shop to buy a Mars Bar and handed one with a clue fastened to it.

Usually our cousins would stay at our grandparents' on Gowan Terrace in Jesmond, a large house with plenty of rooms. Every Sunday afternoon we walked the 2-3 miles through

Jesmond Dene to visit 'Grandma's. Grandpa also lived there but was more in the background, hidden behind his pipe smoke and newspaper.

Walking to our grandparents' house with my mother and siblings I felt indestructible. There would be a lot of laughter on the way as everyone sparked off each other. Our tea at "Grandma's" was a buffet of sandwiches and cakes which I painstakingly arranged in attractive patterns on plates. After tea, Ruth and I would head upstairs to the attic, which was full of old furniture and mattresses that we made into dens or an assault course. If cousin Mark was up he would always join in, and sometimes Alex would pay a visit to see what was going on.

Around 7 pm we gathered around the TV, some of us perched on the end of the sofa, to watch the latest TV drama; 'Last of the Mohicans', 'John Brown's Schooldays', 'Pollyanna' or suchlike. After the 9 o'clock news Grandpa would kindly drive us all home after fetching gifts of Cadbury's Chocolate Flakes, Fruit Gums or Milky Ways. Before getting into the car, if it was a clear sky, I'd stretch my head back and gaze at the stars, trying to imagine what was out there and where the sky ended. It would blow my young mind, but the universe would always be a source of fascination to me.

My sister and I had a mutual friend called Milly who lived around the corner at the top of our street. Her mother, Irena, was Polish; she was flamboyant and dramatic in her attire and her behaviour. Their house was large with many storeys, equipped with all the latest mod cons. Cork tiles ran throughout the downstairs so you were told to take your shoes off at the front door. Antique furniture and huge plants filled the living room. I was a regular visitor there, sometimes staying for tea. Their fridge was filled with intriguing foodstuff; jars of snails, pickled peppers and cheese with holes; white gingerbread biscuits in the shape of stars. The kitchen smelt of garlic and spices. Irena was always kind and generous to me. I think she felt my quiet composure was a good influence on her hedonistic daughter. Milly was slightly older than my sister and hugely entertaining. Her mother was often trying to get her to do things she didn't want to do, but I never felt uncomfortable around them; it was more camaraderie than argument. Milly had a secret crush on my brother Alex. In later years she confessed to watching him adoringly from the upstairs window, as he walked our Red Setter past her house, their manes wafting behind them, oblivious to the secret admirer.

On Saturdays Milly and Tracey, from around the other corner, sometimes joined my sister and me to help Tom the Milkman with his deliveries. We were lucky to have such experiences before the world became health and safety mad, as it is now, and yet terrible things still happen to children today despite the tight controls. Anyway Tom was a lovely man. He looked like Sid James from the Carry On films. He was a gentle man with a constant smile etched onto his craggy face. We rode up and down the streets on the back of his milk float, exchanging the coloured tokens from the doorsteps for milk bottles. I loved picking up the rare orange tokens for sterilised milk, whatever that was. The highlight of the morning was when Tom drove us down a steep hill called Matthew Bank. He ended his round at Davidson's Cottages where elderly residents rewarded us with sweets, hopefully not Edinburgh Rock because no-one liked it.

***

Alex continued to be fearless and adventurous as he grew older, and aged only 15 he nearly died. Still in our pajamas, my sister and I were carrying on in our bedroom jumping on our beds when our mother appeared at the door. She explained that Alex had fallen out of a tree and she needed to take him to hospital, and calmly told us to get dressed and wait for her return. We were struck silent with fear and guilt for messing about so late in the day. Acrobatic Alex had climbed about forty feet up a tree and proceeded to somersault around the branch which snapped with his weight, and he landed on the fence below. As his luck would have it, he fell right opposite the Harveys, who were good friends. What's more, Mrs Harvey was a nurse and off duty that day. She rushed out to see to him, whilst one of her lads was sent up to our house.

Alex had broken a number of ribs and punctured his left lung; the hospital gave him a 1 in 5 chance to live. I was only 10 at the time and couldn't stop worrying about him. A few days later it was a relief to finally visit him in hospital.

On arrival at his bedside my face crumpled into tears, and Alex tried to make me laugh and reassure me he would be okay. Amazingly he was. I remember seeing a young lad in the bed next to him who had been in a car accident and could barely move. I was mesmerised as he held a hand in the air and was moving his fingers around. Slowly I realised he was just rolling a bogey.

When they first took Alex into hospital, my Mam stayed with him. They removed his clothes and found a packet of 10 Regal Kingsize cigarettes down his underpants, the proof she had been seeking that he had started smoking. Not that she cared, with her son's life hanging in the balance, she was more amused than annoyed. It wasn't too long before Alex was safely back home. Unfortunately he never stopped smoking though.

***

My mother taught my sister and me how to cook and bake from a young age. We would help make her famous cheese scones and lemon curd. As I grew older, I was allowed to bake alone but before then I could make "Kunzel Cake" because it didn't require any cooking. It was very simple and made from broken digestive biscuits that were smashed in a bag with a rolling pin then mixed into melted golden syrup and butter, pressed into a tin and cooled in the fridge. Christmas was a time for much baking. The Christmas cake was made a month or so earlier, and everyone in the family had to give it a lucky stir. Robert would tell the same joke every year whilst the cake was being made;

"Mother, mother can I lick the bowl out? The mother replies, no of course you can't. Just pull the chain like everyone else".

Witty remarks ricocheted around our house. Comedy was part of our life, a learned response to relieving tension. Morecambe and Wise were the most popular comedians at the time. We even had a family come round to watch it with us on our black and white television. My mother had known the Donalds since her youth. Their father, Jimmy, was a naturally funny man and it appeared to run in the family. Humour was a staple ingredient for all of us.

Occasionally the Findleys would come to stay, which would take hilarity to a new level. Liz Findley and my mother had bared their souls to each other a long time ago and visits would be marked by long periods of hysterical laughter between the two of them. They shared a unique view of life that relied on a fairly black sense of humour, which saw them through their trials and tribulations.

One afternoon Robert walked in on them crying with laughter as they read out the obituaries from the local newspaper.

"How could you find that funny - they're grieving?" He was horrified by them which only made them lose control more. It was the dreadfully banal yet flowery wording they were howling at. Liz and my Mam were adept at devising stories about people which would amuse them for hours.

One Christmas, in order to fit Liz and her two sons in, I had to share the dog's bed which was the bottom of Alex's bunk bed. Red was a handsome Red Setter and about the same size as me at the time. He was a much loved addition to the family. He came to us aged 3 because a mother at my Mam's nursery came in one day very distressed, crying that her husband had told her the dog would be put to sleep as they couldn't afford to keep him. It was a genuine surprise that my Mam decided to have him, because she said it was for Alex's birthday but Alex had never made a big deal of wanting a dog, so I think there was more to it. We wondered if he had been abused by a man. When Ken, a friend of the family, called round and met him for the first time Red responded aggressively. Ken was tall and dark haired with a big heart and a firm manner and he engaged both to placate Red and win him over. He was fine with men after that.

Red brought a heap of joy. Every Christmas I'd get him a large bone from the local butcher along the road. Such was his temperament he'd allow me to take the bone off him to scrape out the juicy marrow and feed it to him with my fingers. He was a beautiful and intelligent animal; we even played hide and seek with him.

Christmas morning was an agonising wait whilst my mother insisted on washing up the breakfast dishes before opening any presents under the tree. We weren't spoilt and my mother was careful with money, but there were plenty of thoughtful presents. I witnessed her putting money in an envelope which she later passed to the bin men and was struck by her generosity.

Christmas dinner itself was magnificent. The dining table was dressed to impress, laden with an enormous turkey, vegetables and trimmings, cooked with experience and basted in love. Colourful condiments enjoyed annual residence in festive tableware. Our foam placemats from childhood, shaped as a cat, monkey, robin and a fish with big, pink lips were brought out, along with the solid silver, napkin rings to mark the special day. A glass jar of mini homemade meringues sat on the sideboard in delicate pink and white that were sublimely chewy in the centre.

My mother was happy when she spent time with Liz. She had devoted her life to looking after the four of us and gave no time and energy to finding a new partner. In fact, I'm not convinced she was interested anymore. After having her heart broken, it was never going to be easily offered to anyone again, so we were the focus of her love. Sometimes after going to bed and getting up to use the bathroom, I'd hear the dulcet tones of Long John Baldry emanating from the living room entwined with the smoke from an occasional Silk Cut. My Mam had a lot of joy in her life and laughed a lot, sometimes until she cried.

With Liz staying it was like having another mother in tow. There was no point in trying to slip anything past these two, they sang from the same hymn sheet as far as parenting went. Alex and Douglas, Liz's eldest son, were a dastardly pair when they were brought together. One Christmas they polished off the remains of the turkey in the early hours of Boxing Day and blamed it on Red. Liz and my mother shared the belief that children were little people with their own lives, desires, thoughts and responsibilities. They didn't seek to find their self worth through their children's lives and this gave us a real freedom of expression and a confidence to be who we were. We weren't an exclusive tribe and there was usually someone's friend visiting or staying over, and they were always offered food and made welcome.

We thrived on making each other laugh. Alongside board games of Monopoly, Cluedo and Escape from Colditz, new leisure activities were devised that we could all participate in and they were free. Very popular was the table tennis tournament played on the dining room table with Liz on the piano. She was an accomplished pianist and the faster she played the quicker you had to hit the ping pong. So to win it, was just as necessary to maintain composure as to play well.

***

Most winters in the seventies it would snow quite heavily and the Valley became the place for sledging. The main slope, which was the steepest, became polished into black ice by the sledges. Ruth and I would share a sledge, and sometimes we would get spun on the way down. If you were really daring you would slide down the black ice standing up. Everyone was there, even little Crispin from the posh bit aged about 5 years old, the only child to arrive on skis, much to our amusement. The blanket of snow prolonged the light, so you only went home when you couldn't feel your fingers anymore.

In contrast to the winter holiday, but equally enjoyable, were the summer visits to a beach called Embleton, north of Newcastle. Reached by car, courtesy of Grandpa, complete with picnic, courtesy of Grandma, this was a special place. The family owned a small beach hut which housed everything we needed; stripey, picnic chairs, cutlery, crockery and a small, wooden boat which pulled along on string. To get there we traversed the golf course, crossed a charming wooden bridge and headed into the dunes, zig zagging along slim, sandy pathways surrounded by elephant grass that whipped your bare legs and left them itchy. This was somewhere it seemed everyone could relax. Adults enjoyed a sheltered and beautiful outlook in front of the hut, looking out to sea, whilst maintaining a bird's eye view of us young folk down on the vast sandy beach.

This beach was never crowded even at the height of summer, the majority of people in the North East preferring to cram onto the likes of Tynemouth and Whitley Bay to access the "delights" of chips, amusement arcades and giant sugar dummies, perhaps. We visited other beaches in Northumberland and the Isle of Wight, but

Embleton was the most special.   We stayed in Spittal near Berwick a few times, hiring a large caravan situated on the top of a hill which crossed the train tracks and led down to the beach. Near the bottom of the hill was an amusement arcade we frequented throughout the holiday, where a significant incident took place one day.

I was about 8 and my mother was in the arcade too. I noticed a girl with Down's syndrome. She looked the same age as me but much bigger. She stood very close to us then suddenly lunged at my mother's neck with both hands. I was fiercely protective, especially of my mother, and became alarmed, but my Mam just stood calmly and smiled. She understood immediately the girl was greatly perturbed that the top button on my mother's blouse was undone and had taken it upon herself to fasten it. My Mam thanked her and I stood there digesting the lesson.

My mother was a special woman with an incredible understanding of children, especially those with a greater need for love and guidance. It's no wonder she was a nurse and then a much loved nursery school teacher. A psychic once told her she had lights around her head that were children who had died and wanted to be around her. My Mam was very pragmatic. She showed no interest in spiritual matters and certainly wasn't religious, but she accepted the remark gracefully.

With five people, a cat and a dog to feed, the weekly shop was very much a Big Shop. My Mam had a close friend called Ellen who lived nearby with her husband Ken, the man who had won Red's trust. On Friday evening she would pick us up in her car to take us to the supermarket.

Every Saturday we visited the library, a round building in the heart of Jesmond. Everyone in the family read, but Robert and my Mam were prolific. I would head over to the children's section sometimes with my sister. It took me ages to pick out a book or two, and I marvelled at how my Mam could choose books for any of us who couldn't make it. After the library, we'd head over to the Co-op and Laws Stores. Alex had a Saturday job there and would bring home "luxuries" like sachets of cod in cheese sauce that were separated from their glossy boxes.

On the corner stood an amazing delicatessen called Leithards. It had a seriously high counter and an array of specialist food and drink. Items were positioned around the sides in tiers, like punters at a stadium, quirky shaped bottles containing exotic fruit suspended in brandy, German biscuits and fancy chocolates. Each Christmas, my Mam treated herself to a box of Terry's chocolate gingers from Santa.

Further along was the Co-op where we bought the weekly shop. Two things caught my attention here. Firstly the green shield stamps you earned with your shop, that I stuck into a puffy, paper book. The second was the kindly man on the till who wore thick, dark glasses that made his eyes look tiny .

The final stop was the chippy on Brentwood Avenue for fish and chips, though I had a cheese pasty and Alex opted for a mince pie.

I remember one lady in particular who wore a snug, grey bun on top of the kindest looking face. After the longest wait, I watched them above the counter skillfully throwing our order into tight, newspaper parcels. We headed straight home with them so they would still be hot.

Most of the time we created our own entertainment and it was normally free, but once a year there was an event that we always went to as a family. Incorporating excitement and a little danger, it was Europe's largest travelling fair. The fair arrived in June and made Newcastle Town Moor its home for a week. It was enormous with every kind of ride to spin and tip and scare the living daylights out of you. Colourful stalls, dripping with bags of goldfish and gigantic teddy bears, impossible to win, stood in rows from one end of the fair to the other, each stall manned by Gypsies with sharp eyes and charismatic banter to lure you in. The aroma of Candy floss, fried onions and damp straw filled your nostrils. There were bizarre sideshows claiming to show you the smallest, tallest and most grotesque, but my Mam never wasted her precious money on them. I kept my eyes peeled for dropped coins and was rarely disappointed.

The whole family visited for one special night. As we got older, our mother would just take Ruth and myself. Alex made his own way with his friends and girlfriends, sometimes letting us tag along. I don't think Robert was that interested as long as he got a toffee apple brought back. Ruth was always more daring than me and frequently pulled me out my comfort zone onto faster, scarier rides like the Space Rockets and the Mexican Hat. I preferred the Meteorite, a giant spinning cage with people strapped around the sides. It rose up and slowly tilted on its axis whilst spinning round faster and faster. It looked much scarier than it was. Being small I could wriggle up the side off the metal floor and the centrifugal force would plaster me against the cage wall. My Mam was always watching and waving from below, laden with coats and prizes. After a circuit of the fairground, we headed out past the Helter Skelter and the donkeys we'd ridden earlier, across the field to home, scooping up coconuts and a toffee apple for my Mam and Robert.

In time, Robert, complete with his dark, shoulder length hair and Afghan coat, headed off to University, and Alex exchanged his Harrington and Fred Perry T shirt for a Royal Navy uniform and a crew cut. This left three of us in the house along with Jane the cat and Red the dog. For the first time in a long time my Mam had a little more money in her pocket. This allowed her to splash out on a wall-to-wall carpet for the hall and living room, and take my sister and me to Butlins in Yorkshire. All was well in the world.

The Game changer

In 1977 when Rose was 11 years old she had a vivid nightmare:- *It was like a film and the camera flitted between dark portraits of elderly strangers in a darkened gallery, getting faster and faster. The background music lent a sinister edge to the nightmare and increased in speed and pitch, reaching a crescendo as the camera zoomed in and suddenly halted on the vision of a coffin. I realised to my horror that the coffin contained the body of my beloved mother.*

I woke up distressed, and Ruth, my sister, with whom I shared a bedroom, knew this wasn't an ordinary nightmare. She put the Big light on and took me downstairs to where our mother was watching television.

I didn't want to tell her what the nightmare was about but she insisted. An almost imperceptible wave of shock flitted over my mother's face as I completed the description of the terrifying end scene and this perturbed me far more than the nightmare itself. However she comforted me, and I went back to bed and never thought of it again. Approximately one year later my mother was dead.

She knew at the time of my nightmare that her health wasn't good as she had suffered a second stroke. She knew the next one might be the last, as her own mother had died of the same thing. I was blissfully ignorant.

Tragically she did suffer another stroke.

Ruth bravely rang the doctor under instruction from our mother who was experiencing an intense stabbing pain behind her left eye and had to lie in her bed. When the ambulance came to take her to hospital she played it down, but I insisted on giving her a needy hug. My appetite had vanished, so Red gratefully ate my discarded toast and peanut butter.

She remained in hospital, and we visited her once. Annoyingly, a teacher from her work was visiting at the same time, which meant our precious time with our mother was sabotaged. A few days later we were waiting patiently to be taken to visit her again. We were staying at our Great Aunty Wyn's with family. It was sickening to watch the grandfather clock go past the time we were meant to be collected. Eventually our Aunty Alison arrived back from the hospital. She took my sister and me into the next room, gathered us around her, and gently told us our mother had died.

That year I'd bought my Mam a Busy Lizzie plant for Mother's Day. It was a sweet, little thing but grew into a huge and beautiful plant, taking pride of place on the dining room mantelpiece. Shortly after my mother died it also died and turned into a sad, brown mush.

Losing my mother at the age of 12 was like the sun being taken from the sky. The worst thing imaginable had actually happened. When I was 9 years old I went to see Bambi at the cinema with my family for my birthday . The young deer spends all his time with his mother learning about the world and being nurtured. He doesn't know his father very well so he is particularly attached to his mother. Later in the film, when he is still a fawn, his mother is tragically shot dead by a hunter. I was devastated when this happened and inconsolable, I know I was a sensitive kid, but maybe I resonated with it, knowing on some level it was going to happen to me, or it was it just my deepest fear? I had the same response when I watched a scene in a Cowboy Western which had a scene where a 12 year old boy stood frozen in fear at campfire staring at a large spider sitting in a cooking pot. He had just been told that his mother was dead. Children react differently from adults in grief. I was taken to the doctor with a sore throat as I couldn't speak. It was a phantom illness; I just didn't want to speak. Plenty of people say thoughtless and stupid things or treat you like a pariah because *they* don't know what to say but think they *should say something*. It was an unreal time, and as a child I had little control over what was happening and what was being arranged for the future. I found out years later that the Findleys in Scotland, Ellen and Ken in Newcastle and our mother's brother in Australia offered to take me and my sister, so our lives could have followed many paths. However, my father insisted we went to live with him and our stepmother.

To compound the already seismic loss, I was told by my Dad that I would have to put our cat to sleep because our stepmother was allergic to animals, and we couldn't take her or our dog with us. She wasn't an easy cat to pass on to someone but she was in perfect health and I'm sure someone could have taken her in. I prayed for Jane not to return home so that it didn't have to happen, and I was sick to my stomach at the prospect. It fell to poor Ellen to take me and Jane to a "cat lady" in Jesmond to be euthanised.   There were loads of cats running around her house; she was a big, jolly lady, like a dark-haired Diana Dors. She didn't put Jane to sleep whilst we were there, so I wondered years later if this buxom lady had a little space in her big heart to squeeze Jane in. Alex arranged for Red to be given away to the Harveys down the street.

***

Life couldn't be any worse. I recall thinking that maybe a miracle could happen and my mother could come back to life, but after the first week I knew it wasn't going to happen. Alex and a close friend of his took Ruth and me on the train to Spanish City, a resident fairground at the coast, to try and put a smile on our faces. I think he did manage to get a smile out of us, but then children have the capacity to push grief right down, and deal with it much later, or not. I know something shut down for me that day and maybe likewise for my siblings. It was the end of one life and the start of a very different one. My treasured memories of the years spent with my mother would remain imbued with a golden glow.

Jimmy, my mother's old and dear friend, was kind enough to take my Mam's clothes to charity shops. Other people were involved in sorting through the remainder of our house. Unfortunately some things were given away without any consultation or simply disappeared. A lot of our childhood possessions were lost. Years later when I was in my twenties I had a vivid dream that I returned to our much loved home. It wasn't an ordinary dream; everything was "cast" with a grey hue and I always dream in colour. I floated into every single room of the house and viewed everything exactly as it had been back then. I savoured every second of the experience, moving up close and hovering over all kinds of items that even I had forgotten about. Ruth had been given a couple of wooden plaques one birthday that had stood at either end of the white mantle piece in our bedroom; one of a girl and one of a boy, painted in bright colours and highly varnished, and I could see every detail. It was an immensely healing experience and really helped me with the loss.

***

Our father's affair in North London morphed into a second marriage and produced a stepmother. I'm sure she didn't think in her wildest dreams she would have two teenage stepdaughters entering her life with our Dad, following the premature death of his first wife. However that is always a possibility when you get involved with a married man. Dazed and vacant, Ruth and I were driven down to East Sussex by our Dad to start our new life with them in the sleepy, remote countryside. Our brothers

Robert and Alex had fledged already, but we were being dropped into the nest of a rival bird which was something none of us wanted. To add to the already strained relationships our stepmother was pregnant with her first child. Ruth and I knew we would have to stick together to get through it. She was chalk to my cheese, but we had a close bond made even stronger by our shared loss and survival instinct.

We attended the local school in the next village, catching the school bus every day. With our age difference we were placed in separate years. However there was an occasion not long after we started when we were both pulled out of our classes by the Deputy Head, Miss Upchurch. She was a tall lady with a grey-haired bob that swished when she spoke. Her pointed, haughty face was matched perfectly by her posh accent and she said "jolly" quite a lot.

"Now, I've a surprise for you both, Mum's been in today", she announced. Ruth and I looked at each other in amazement. For a couple of wonderful seconds it seemed magically possible that she was still alive, and we both felt it.

"She has dropped off something for you ....", her voice rambled on in the background as we slowly realized she was referring to our stepmother. It was incredibly thoughtless of the teacher not to pick her words more carefully. Sadly we weren't allowed to attend our mother's funeral, which meant there was no real closure. Our father was probably being overprotective when he made that decision, but it also meant we didn't get to see all the people who loved her and feel their support.

It took a long time for us to make connections in East Sussex, with slow speaking southerners who said "Watcha!" and played a stupid game called Stoolball that we'd never played before. Our hearts were heavy and we missed our brothers whom we only saw occasionally when they came to visit us. It was not a happy home; there was too much resentment and conflicting agendas clashing loudly together. We did our best though and often escaped on our bikes to seek adventure. The village bus ran once an hour which was ridiculous compared with what we were used to in the city. We were fed, though often hungry, and had clothes bought for school but little else, so we stole fashionable clothing regularly so as not to stand out. I nicknamed Ruth "Raffles" because she was so good at it. We were never caught.

A big turning point came when Ruth came home from a German exchange with a Simon and Garfunkel' album under her arm and cigarettes in her pocket. We sat around the record player and sang along to it for hours. Ruth had started to forge her own future and it was destined to have a rebellious seam running through it. Cider was discovered around the age of 14 years old so that opened things up for us, as village pubs were very relaxed about the age law.

We eventually made some good friends at school but I still relied on my big sister for a lot.

We both found a few families who 'adopted us', inviting us for tea and sleep overs. Ruth had a close friend who lived on a farm and was one of six twins! We both spent a lot of time with that family; with eight round their farmhouse table, another two didn't seem to make a lot of difference. We were obsessed with netball and were often excused from classes to join our teams to play against schools all over the South East.

***

After three years, Ruth left school and returned to Newcastle upon Tyne to attend college. I felt very alone and had to cope with a year on my own until I could return home to Newcastle at the age of sixteen. However my salvation was my step-brother Lachlan who was born a couple of months after we first arrived. I wasn't really interested when he was a baby, but once he could walk and talk he was a source of great joy. I loved spending time with him; he was a really sweet child. There was a lot of opportunity to take him out on my own, as it suited my stepmother to use me for babysitting so that she could work. When I was about 15 years old I took him to Hastings for the day by bus which took a good few hours. We blew bubbles at the back of the bus with a toy consisting of a straw and a tube of sticky stuff which kept him amused on the journey.

When we arrived I headed to the amusement arcade which I knew was there from a previous visit with Ruth. I wanted to show him the giant one-armed bandit called Big Ben. I had brought his pushchair and remember making my way purposefully along the pavement. I was confused by the hostile expressions I was getting. As a self-conscious teenager I was used to feeling uncomfortable around strangers, but it was years later that I realised people must have thought he was my child and they were passing their misguided judgement on what they presumed was a teenage mother!

In 1982, the Falklands War was in full swing. Alex was still in the Navy and I was anxious about him getting drafted but thankfully the war ended before he was sent there. Years later he told me that on his way there he had been throwing a heavy bag of rubbish overboard when he lost his footing and went over with it. Miraculously for him someone saw him go over and alerted the Captain. He was on a Frigate which takes a long time to turn round, so he had to wait patiently in the water before they scooped him up to safety. Alex was like a cat with nine lives.

In a couple of months I'd be heading back to Newcastle to study Hotel Management at Newcastle College, but before I left I was invited to go on holiday with my close friend Shelley whose house I'd stayed at many times. Her parents were Scottish and oozed warmth and generosity. They were driving to North West France and staying in a house with a couple they knew well. I was so excited to be going on holiday, and they insisted we took our bikes. Shelley and I put a lot of effort into making each other laugh, we did impersonations of people we knew and played about, perfecting accents. We recorded a radio show on a cassette and sent it between ourselves for our amusement. It was great fun clowning around, and I felt her parents were very fond of me, as I was of them.

Most days we headed out into the French country side on our bikes and explored the village. Having a car meant her parents could take us further afield. There was a lake nearby and the sea wasn't too far away. One day we drove to the beach and headed into the water. The waves were huge, and we were having great fun jumping in them as they crashed past and on to the shore. It was a glorious sunny day; however there was a red flag on show which we failed to heed.

I'm in the sea off the North West coast of France and suddenly the idyllic summer holiday with my friend and her family takes a sinister turn. A few minutes prior I was revelling in the boisterous ocean with Shelley and her Dad, Cameron, but the Atlantic Ocean means business today and has turned angry at our hedonistic dismissal of the red flag impaled on the beach. I'm not a strong swimmer and Cameron, is as far out as me and starting to have difficulty swimming, which strikes a desperate blow to my diminishing confidence. Cameron was having an asthma attack and was really struggling to breathe, never mind swim.

The enormous swell is lurching me up and forward then pulling me further back out to sea. Two steps forward, four steps back. I am taking in mouthfuls of seawater and struggling to breathe. Very soon I am completely exhausted and resigning myself to giving up. The hope becomes unbearable and the battle to reach land seems futile in the face of this mighty sea. It was at exactly this point that the fear and panic dissolved entirely, and to my surprise I "watched" my body going under the waves whilst the real "me" began to rise slowly upwards for about a third of my body length. In the next few minutes, or was it seconds, I experienced a lot of things which in retrospect would seem hard to fit into such a short space of time, like a scene from Alice in Wonderland. My life started scrolling past my eyes on an imaginary film reel beginning with an image of me as a toddler, playing in the garden of our East Finchley home. I *nearly* saw a newspaper article which described how a 16 year old English girl had tragically drowned off the West coast of France. I say nearly, because it didn't commit itself entirely to print but was a fleeting image in my mind. Finally, and most wonderfully, I actually ***became*** part of the sky. It wasn't possible to fall down from my lofty viewpoint as I knew without any doubt that the true me ***was*** the sky, ***and*** the earth and ***everything around me***. I was filled with absolute joy, peace, freedom and an expanded understanding of how it is, no worry and an immense desire to just "be". I could "see" the beach and all the people on it, including the brave young French boy who swam out to drag Cameron back to safety. I knew categorically; when you drown you don't go down, you go up.

41

Suddenly smashing into my awareness was the sound of Shelley's mother.

"You *can* make it Rose",

Shelley herself was reaching out her arm to try and grasp the fingers of my outstretched hand, and somehow, eventually, we made contact. She told me afterwards she was well out of her depth too. I was totally wiped out and helped out of the water onto the sand. I couldn't believe I had survived, as a part of me had expected to drown.

The significance of this event wasn't apparent at the time but, as I carried on through my life I realised that this near death experience was a turning point in my understanding of death, and altered my belief that when you die you remain in a dark, lonely place, frozen in time with no-one and nothing around you. This was where I had believed my mother resided.

Transition

The walls of the hospital room slip away and
reveal a beautiful light that fills every cell in her
body with a sensation of deep calm. It dissolves
the pain in her head and the dreadful exhaustion
she finally succumbed to. Familiar looking faces
emit love and kindness surrounds her. The feeling
of peace is sublime. In a flash Margaret is
whisked supersonically through the air, caressed
by an unseen intelligence. Memories from the
span of her life drift up from her consciousness
then fall away like scales. The image of her four
children comes wooshing into her thoughts, and
the emotion is so intense it feels like a blow to her
head. This process continues for some time and
she feels looser and lighter as she travels faster and
faster through rainbow colours, each colour
cleansing away fear and sadness and leaving an
increasing sensation of pure joy.

Time doesn't make any sense; days may
have passed, but it also feels like only seconds ago
she was lying in the hospital bed. Eventually there
is a slowing down and a golden, shimmering light
pervades. The light has consciousness and
intelligence, speaking directly to her without
words. Margaret watches as human shapes step
out from the light and move towards her. She is
greeted by her mother and father who died 29
years ago; she has never seen them look so well.
Her being is infused with their deep love for her.
She is transported with her mother and father to
the Taj Mahal in India. She is full of wonder at the

exquisite beauty and the serene waters. She had always wanted to visit there but didn't come close in her lifetime. In fact she did very little travelling, having dedicated her life to nurturing her children and other parents' children. It is truly magnificent.

Her parents explain to her that she has died and that they are all together again and everything is going to be okay. There is nothing for her to worry about. Her children will be looked after and she will be able to see them soon, but for now she needs to rest, and this is a good place for that to happen. The bench she is sitting on gently dissolves into a large and luxurious bed that wouldn't look out of place in a five star hotel, and, as the exotic images around her slowly fade, she slips easily into a deep coma.

***

During the deep sleep she dreams someone is calling out her name. It's not a voice she recognises, but it has authority and urgency so she "wakes up". An angelic face with a radiant smile is looking down at her from her bedside. The room is bathed in a celestial, golden light. She has a sense of enormous wings wafting a cooling breeze over her face.

We must go now Margaret, she whispers.

Margaret is entranced with the beautiful creature and feels safe. They "fly" off into a black, velvet sky covered with stars like a giant pin cushion studded with shiny, silver dots. They pick up speed then begin to dive down. The sky starts to lighten and eventually settles on summer-day-blue. Land is swirling past, a palette of green and yellow. They slow down and she can clearly see a coastline and a vast ocean, then a beach with a couple of bright, red flags in the sand.

They approach the sea but there is no sense of fear. It would be impossible to fall as she is part of the atmosphere so there is nowhere to fall to. She sees another angelic being in the water about the size of three men. It is radiating circles of emerald green light which dissipate over the large and ominous waves, but doesn't seem to be wet. As they draw near she can see it is holding a man in the sea who is struggling to breathe; a young man is swimming out towards him'

Something compels her to look over to the right. There in the middle of the sea about 100 yards from the rescue scene is someone else struggling to swim. As the wave breaks and a head appears she realises with horror it is her 16 year old daughter Rose. The angel at her side beams an enormous green light onto the drowning adolescent, and in milliseconds they are lifting her body up in the water so she doesn't drown. Margaret understands instinctively that she needs to concentrate her love for Rose and maintain a focus of courage and strength as she knows her daughter is tiring. The angel is manipulating time, slowing it down to enable them to maximise help for Rose, keeping her head above the water and enabling her to reach her friend's outstretched hand.

A palpable peace descends on Margaret as

she watches her daughter swim slowly in to the safety of the shore. She looks over and sees the man has been rescued too.

It is time to leave, whispers the angel.

Margaret steals a hug with Rose which feels wonderful. In those seconds she is able to feel her daughter's emotions, which are a mixture of exhaustion and shock because she expected to drown. The embrace sends a wave of calm over Rose. Margaret is tiring, so the angel scoops her up under her wing and they head back into the darkness and the stars. Rescue complete.

Ch ch ch changes

Whilst living in East Sussex I became close friends with a girl called Cherry, who lived in the same village, down the road in a converted Oast house. Cherry's response to her coarse ginger hair was to cut it short and sculpt it into a feature with no hint of apology. She was athletic and hyperactive, and cut a cool figure in her androgynous, black clothing. Cherry was an original.

Shelley and Cherry also knew each other from school, and Shona from Scotland was also in our discerning little group. We got on well because we shared a love of the absurd and enjoyed mimicking teachers. Occasionally we'd go out for a meal or to a disco. There wasn't a great range of activities in the middle of nowhere, but parents were very obliging with lifts.

All of us were on the cusp of exploding into the world of boyfriends and crushes. Shortly before I left for Newcastle, Shelley and Cherry were over at mine as I had the place to myself. Cherry brought round a vinyl record she'd just purchased ,entitled [4]Aladdin Sane.

"Can I put this on?" she announced gleefully, whilst already heading to the record player.

"What is it?" I enquired.

" David Bowie of course", she exclaimed as I nodded permission.

The track began with a hypnotic beat that grew louder, and when the singing commenced she started to mime the lyrics perfectly and sensually.

She was mesmerising. Shelley was smirking, but I was utterly transfixed and decided there and then I wanted to walk through the door into the world of David Bowie.

I wonder if something happens the first time music reaches into you, a cosmic reaction with the rushing hormones and a myriad of questions buzzing around a teenage mind. A number of artists could light the fuse, but as with all good love affairs, timing is everything, and for me it was David Bowie and it would last a lifetime.

I was sad to leave my good friends; they had helped me cope with the 4 years I had spent in a place where I had felt like an outsider. Their humour and friendship had been a life saver and I would never forget it. However, it was time to fly true north where I could stay with my Grandpa who lived alone now after Grandma sadly died a year before my mother.

***

I can't describe the intoxicating freedom of leaving the confines of school and the oppression of an unhappy household. I was sixteen years old and there was no-one to tell me what to do. My main priority was to work through the back catalogue of David Bowie records. Not having a father around always made me feel different, and then losing my mother at the age of 12 was another reason to feel outside of the norm. David Bowie made an art of *being* different and he was *very* inspiring. He walked his walk and talked his talk. I remember seeing him perform on Top of the Pops when I was about seven years old and was bewildered by him in his strange clothes and bright coloured hair.

His lyrics brought the guidance and understanding I was looking for. I felt like an alien moving from the urban North East to the rural South East with a family shattered by grief. He spoke of aliens and his lyrics exposed a personal understanding of loneliness and sadness I could relate to. He shared his heartache of lost love but also captured the thrill of sexual attraction. There were no rules in his world, but plenty of glamour and individuality.

I reconnected with two old school friends, Ava and Carla who I'd known since I was five years old, and they became my anchor. Their friendships continued through my life like golden threads, sometimes wearing thin when we lived apart but never breaking off, and subsequently strengthening, like steel over the years.

Ava had her own gang from school, mainly lads; they were intelligent and funny and treated Ava with respect. I fitted in well, comfortable with the platonic vibe. Ava was in a relationship with one of the guys called Jack who was well liked by everyone, they were a popular couple. Jack was very upbeat and more often than not had a smile on his face about something. We would meet for coffee in town at the Tyneside Cinema. Ava was striking looking and had modelled since she was a child. She was a singer and songwriter too, so as well as going to see her band play we would frequent local haunts in Newcastle to see live bands. Life was a party of drinking, clubbing and experimenting with recreational drugs.

We knocked around together most days, just doing stuff and calling on people. One day Ava suggested we go and see a tarot reader in town she'd heard of, neither of us having seen one before and we were sixteen.

We arrived at the address and were shown in by a woman sporting a moustache who asked us to take a seat on a shabby looking sofa. She sat at her desk scribbling important notes and taking calls to arrange bookings for Joan the medium who was in another room behind a closed door. The assistant wore a harsh expression and looked slightly irritated, so I didn't feel brave enough to ask her anything, despite my head being full of questions. Apparently we wouldn't have long to wait as we were next in and I was first.

I walked in the door and headed slowly towards the lady at the far end of the room sitting at a desk with her chubby arms resting on the top. She was smiling out at me with intense, sparkly eyes. Joan told me that when I walked in the room a lady called Margaret walked in behind me, she stood behind me when I sat down and laid her hands on my shoulders. She told me it was my mother and described her in detail. I was overwhelmed with emotion and the accuracy of her statement. She continued to pass important advice to me, telling me to take every day as a bonus because life on Earth was a gift and one day she would be with me again. She reassured me that she would always look after me and always keep my head above water. I wondered afterwards if this was a reference to my near drowning in France earlier that year. It was all so fascinating. Joan gave me information that nobody knew. She mentioned the day we buried my mother's ashes in the garden of remembrance, and how I wore a party dress covered in roses, which felt wrong but was the nicest outfit I had. She talked about how hard it was to leave us all and how sorry she was to go but there was nothing she could do. The whole reading lasted about half an hour. It was mind boggling; I didn't know what to make of it, but it felt really important.

After Ava's reading we compared them as we walked along the streets towards our respective homes. Ava hadn't lost anyone close so she didn't get messages from anyone in particular; nevertheless she was impressed with the information Joan had given her.

Carla was originally my sister's friend as they were in the same class at school. I'd always got on well with her and we had the same sibling pattern, a sister and two brothers. Nobody had any money then, so it was a common practice for mothers to pass on bags of clothes called hand-me-downs. We received many of these from friends of my mother's friends, and we also passed on clothes to Carla's mother. It was exciting when a new bag arrived, especially if I was the first one to choose. Ruth and I stayed over at Carla's sometimes and she often stayed at ours. We were Girl Guides together so had already amassed many important memories in our short lives. After I returned to Newcastle Ruth left to join the Royal Navy, following in Alex's footsteps.

Carla and I had the opportunity to get to know each other better and forge a deeper friendship. We'd go to a club called Tiffanys on a Monday night, Heavy Metal night. Carla was in love with Robert Plant and David Coverdale and had a huge hippy heart inside her; she always looked out for the underdog and still does. She began travelling when she was fairly young, inspired, perhaps, by her idols from the Sixties music scene. India was one of the first places she trekked and later in life she travelled to every continent on the planet.

It was fantastic to have my childhood friends back in my sphere, but I made new friends easily at college, though deep down I felt a great emptiness. I carried a vacuous hole where my mother had been which I hadn't begun to fill. In fact I was too naive to even know it was there. I am naturally cautious, but at this time I was uncharacteristically fearless. My life over the next few years wasn't going to be easy but neither would it be boring. Without parental parameters I was destined for misadventure.

At college I studied Hotel Management, and as the 2 year course progressed I became increasingly bored with the whole thing. There were some particularly nasty lecturers who didn't help to engage me.

Miss Cleethorpe was a short, round woman with bright red lipstick who favoured a pinstriped suit with an ostentatious, white blouse and stupidly high heels. Her partner in crime was Mr Bennett, a skinny guy with bitchy eyes who fancied himself as a modern day [5]Flashman. Both taught with sarcasm and humiliation. They would single people out for attack if a hairstyle was sloppy or someone's trousers didn't fit. They wouldn't tolerate anyone being a minute late regardless of the reason. They were harsh. I don't believe you learn more this way, but it set me up to work with some proper assholes in the real world. The catering industry does seem to attract more than a few who like to play out their power games in the kitchen or the more public arena of the restaurant. The practical classes were the best and the lecturers there were all really nice. I learnt the basics of nouvelle cuisine which was useful, but I didn't wish to take it any further. It had been a means to an end to get me back home to Newcastle.

The truth was I was far more interested in building up my David Bowie collection than learning how to carry a boiled potato using a fork and spoon. So I'd miss classes, choosing instead to devour the latest vinyl I'd purchased.

I was living at Alex's 3 bedroomed flat with his girlfriend Stevie. Alex was away in the Royal Navy for long stretches, but had his room for when he returned on leave. He enjoyed our friends visiting. Some of them were from my College, including Harry, a handsome Indian Geordie. At college Harry was a charming clown and got away with so much, because of it, I recall he was very polite to my brother and thanked him for allowing us to come and descend on him when he'd just come back from leave, but he loved the company. Alex had an expensive record player and a cool record collection, and more worldly experience than any of us so there was a lot of respect for him. He entertained us all with a musical quiz called "Bits and Pieces" in which you had to guess the names and artists from snippets of songs. Alex had taken hours to create them to entertain the lads on the ship, while they were away.

His girlfriend Stevie was the total opposite of me, but it worked. She loved Boy George and I loved David Bowie. Jane was a soft rock chick and I was a moody alternative. She had blonde hair and blue eyes and I had dark hair and brown eyes, though my hair went through a number of colours, staying with the Ziggy Stardust look for a long time. Her best friend Jamie was part of the package, and she would usually stay over on a Saturday night. Alex came home with a kitten one day and there was strong competition to name him. Fortunately I won, and he was christened Ziggy not Boy George. He was a cute little tabby who became my trusted companion.

***

On 3 July I travelled down to London to join Cherry, her brother and some friends. We had tickets to see David Bowie on his Serious Moonlight Tour thanks to her brother, who was a huge fan with a proper job who'd managed to get hold of them. The following day we saw Bauhaus at the Hammersmith Palais so it was an amazing weekend of music. David Bowie played at Milton Keynes Bowl, the sun shone and the atmosphere was celebratory. The Beat played a great set, and ironically, Icehouse warmed the crowd up perfectly. Finally the man himself appeared. He bounced onto the stage in his lemon yellow suit, boxing and grinning. The audience was vast and crushing; even my neck was sweating I was so hot. It was claustrophobic, so I pushed to the front of the stage to find something to hang on to that wasn't going to move. I couldn't believe that for one special night I would be in the same place as my Idol, David Bowie. He was tanned and energetic and was enjoying himself enormously, a brand new persona for the fans to savour.

"You are colossal!" he shouted to us. It was a humongous show with massive props. He kicked a giant globe out into the audience who dutifully returned it after bouncing it amongst them. Costumes were lavish and the sound rolled across the stadium. As the sky darkened, hundreds of golden moon-shaped balloons spilled out of a huge silvery moon which burst open and floated down to us. I still treasure mine today. During Space Oddity a canopy of polka dot lights appeared above us. At seventeen it was my first major concert and the bar was set forever high.

I teamed up with Cherry again later that year to attend the David Bowie World Convention at the Cunard Hotel in London. The event was peppered with look-a-likes. They showed his films, and people who knew him gave talks, including Ken Pitt, his early manager, who signed my programme. At the end they hosted a disco playing solely David Bowie tracks. It was intense, a David Bowie power shower!

***

The following summer, I finished college. This was it, at the age of 18 I was finally cut free from the constriction of yet another institution. The course I had really wanted to do was Art Foundation at Bath Lane, but I didn't apply as I didn't think I was good enough, which is why I chose Hotel Management. I needed a dead cert course to get me back to Newcastle and away from East Sussex. With that out of the way, I enrolled in a class at Bath Lane that I could casually call in on to build up a portfolio whilst looking for some work. I was also painting at home but they were exclusively David Bowie portraits.

I hadn't managed to secure a job yet, and Ava asked if I wanted to travel around Europe for a few weeks. I said yes immediately. We were on the dole, so we put in a holiday form which would give us a month to travel before having to sign on again. It was the summer of 1984. We met at the Tyneside Cinema and had a proper meal before setting off for the motorway to hitch to North London where we stayed for a few days with a family Ava knew, then on to Europe.

We started and ended our journey in

Amsterdam. In fact on both occasions we stayed longer than planned; it's easy to get stuck there when you're stoned. We met people our age from around the globe and engaged in easy conversations, sharing joints and eating irresistible munchies like chips with peanut butter sauce and mayonnaise. The weather was great, though we spent a lot of time in the Coffee Houses. It was too easy to get lost around the canals, and trying to find a particular place proved tricky. Favourite haunts were the Bulldog and the Goa, the latter we christened "best sofa in the world", having fallen asleep on it for hours. Nobody batted an eyelid. It was Amsterdam.

From there we hitched through Belgium to Paris, then from Paris down to Cannes, over to Genoa and Venice, up to Interlaken in Switzerland and onto Munich.

Ava was trying to hitch a lift in the early hours from the side of a road, in Munich. I was huddled up on the pavement trying to conserve my heat and stay awake. She was braving the cold, and kept warm by dancing; Ava is a great dancer. Whilst we were travelling our luck went up and down all the time. Just when I thought it had finally run out, along comes a lift in a warm and comfortable Mercedes, bingo! The driver was a diplomat and could take us all the way into West Berlin. The roads through to West Berlin were in appalling condition, littered with pot holes. It was no man's land, so neither East nor West Germany took responsibility for their upkeep.

Berlin was the jewel of the trip for me.

Only 4 years previously David Bowie had resided here with his close friend Iggy Pop, I was thrilled to be following in his footsteps.

West Berlin was a cocktail of avant-garde music, striking art and a dash of danger. The Berliners had strong identities. They weren't latching onto the British music scene like the rest of Europe. They indulged their self-expression and were cutting edge, and the danger was real. We visited Checkpoint Charlie and spotted armed guards high up in the towers watching our every move.

Mostly we had been sleeping at railway stations or beaches, and occasionally someone would take us in, but in Berlin we found a cheap guest house which was a luxury. I wrote out my last Euro cheque and forgot it couldn't exceed £50, so my £80 cheque was rendered useless. Fortunately, through the miracle of technology, Ava's Dad cabled some money over. The day after we first arrived we woke up after a deep, recuperative sleep. Our beds had giant, white duvets on them like clouds. We got ready and went out to find some breakfast. As we strolled sleepily along the street observing people's activities, we realised, it wasn't 7 am in the morning, but 7 pm at night. A surreal sensation continued to pervade the trip, as if we were hidden away from the rest of the world like Avalon in the King Arthur Legend. A Canadian couple called Sian and David were also staying at the guest house. We complemented each other perfectly like a perfect picnic. We went out on "family" outings, enjoying the City after sharing a few joints and seeking out secluded night clubs.

We took the subway over to East Berlin. You could get off at a station underground, buy some cheap vodka from a kiosk on the platform and then get back on the train to return to the West, quite clandestine and very appealing to our sense of adventure, as was the whole City. From Berlin we slowly hitched our way back to Amsterdam and eventually on to the ferry home, to sign on.

***

I returned to Berlin, 32 years later and it was a very different place. It's now a huge tourist destination with visitors teeming all over the monuments and museums, one of which is the Wall itself. In my memory I had always pictured Berlin in black and white but it is in full technicolour, albeit from gaudy neon signs that corral tourists towards fast food outlets and entertainment. It still had its edge though, and a sense of free expression.

David Bowie played in Berlin in 1987 as part of a three day festival, along with other British Acts. The concert took place near the Berlin Wall so his music could be heard over in East Germany

"[6]It was one of the most emotional performances I've ever done. I was in tears. They'd backed up the stage to the wall itself so that the wall was acting as our backdrop. We kind of heard that a few of the East Berliners might actually get the chance to hear the thing, but we didn't realize in what numbers they would. And there were thousands on the other side that had come close to the wall. So it was like a double concert where the wall was the division. And we would hear them cheering and singing along from the other side. God, even now I get choked up. It was breaking my heart. I'd never done anything like that in my life, and I guess I never will again. When we did 'Heroes' it really felt anthemic, almost like a prayer."

David Bowie

When David Bowie died in 2016, the German government officially thanked him for bringing down the wall and helping to unify Germany.

GermanForeignOffice

 @GermanyDiplo

[7]Good-bye, David Bowie. You are now among #Heroes. Thank you for helping to bring down the #wall#RIPDavidBowie

10:41 AM - Jan 11, 2016

Orientation

Margaret awoke to joyful music playing around her and the sound of excited voices drifting in through the window. She sensed a lot of activity nearby as if crowds of people were gathering. Something hugely important was about to take place. Her curiosity was lit, and instantly she was outside, dressed and wide awake. As she looked around her she saw people of all ages and cultures, each surrounded with auras of light in different colours and intensities.

One person in particular stood out. He was an old, wise-looking man who wore a shimmering white robe with purple flashes of light that danced around as he walked directly towards her. He had twinkling blue eyes that emitted wisdom and mischief in equal measures.

"Hello Margaret, how wonderful to see you again."

As she looked into his eyes her mind filled instantly with information as if he was still speaking to her.

My name is Orker, I am your guide, and I have followed you every step of your way. You have done really well and achieved great things, I have missed you and I love you dearly.

Everything is okay and as it should be, you have nothing to worry about, it will take some time for you to adjust to the environment but you are home now and we are all very excited to have you back.

His words were deliciously comforting and completely enveloped her, like an apple dipped in

warm toffee. Orker explained that soon she would
receive some guidance and healing that would help
to orientate her. Things were strangely familiar;
she felt she had been here before, albeit a very
long time ago.

Her mother and father appeared behind
him. They both had pink around their heart areas
interspersed with green flashes. Once again
information came telepathically from Orker;
*The different colours represent a special interest
or expertise, for example teaching, healing,
working with animals, working with children,
health, communication, rescue, mental skills, sky,
sea, being, silence, courage, planet, stars, etc.*

She noticed other faces which she couldn't
place, but felt their friendship spanned not just
decades but lifetimes. There was total acceptance
of her, it was family but more so. She knew
without a doubt that everyone loved her and were
overjoyed to have her with them again.

This was Margaret's soul group with whom
she had shared lives for centuries. It's one thing to
go away on holiday and come back and share the
highs and lows of your adventures with friends and
family, but it's another thing entirely to return
from a lifetime. There was some serious catching
up to do, but this would have to wait.

Orker gently drew Margaret to him and
transported her in a second to a large white
building, surrounded by a truly beautiful garden.
The flowers were remarkable in size and hue.
Luminous, yellow blossoms shone like
moonbeams, incandescent orange-red lupins that

were five feet tall, gigantic roses, with sky-blue petals that contained the expansive nature of the sky itself. Deep-purple tulips nodded their wise heads, an actual smile on their faces, and shimmering metallic-green grasses tinkled against each other like wind chimes. The blooms morphed throughout the spectrum, swaying with the pure joy of being. There was nothing like this on Earth.

The building had four magnificent, marble pillars at the front with golden ivy spiralling up. Delicate bluebirds darted across an azure sky, swooping in and out of the building. Their hypnotic song resonated around the cavernous foyer which was made from a translucent material that was pure white. Light seemed to emanate from the walls.

There was much activity. New arrivals accompanied by their guides were to-ing and fro-ing across the vast floor. Around the sides were small booths radiating green light the colour of a summer meadow. Orker led Margaret towards a booth.

There wasn't a door, but suddenly they were inside, cocooned in their own private space, no longer able to hear the birds. Margaret lay on a cushioned bed that quickly moulded around her and supported her head and back perfectly. On the wall in front of her was a large screen.

She looked at the screen and saw that her life was being projected on to it. It began with her arrival into the world as a baby and slowly spanned between significant moments where she'd made important decisions or changed the course of her life significantly. Unlike an ordinary film, this was real. Orker explained how she could stop the process with a thought and tune into the scenes themselves to gain a deep understanding of how everyone was affected by her actions, to consider whether she would have done anything differently. She could look at the situation from anyone's point of view. Margaret grasped that she could view a particular age or event just by thinking about it. Further more, she was shown the consequences of choosing alternative action.

The point of the exercise was to see how her own actions had affected others throughout her life; it wasn't a test but an aid to her spiritual growth, an opportunity to experience the joy and compassion she had brought to so many, to understand how the difficulties she had dealt with had made her grow on a soul level. Some of the events were emotionally challenging, so Orker maintained a protective shield of unconditional love around her throughout.

She could return to the task at any time in the future and take as long as she needed. However it would need to be completed before she could decide what she wanted to focus on next in her soul development.

Take your time to review your life Margaret. You can come back to it many times before completing it.

She was enthralled, and zoomed backwards and forward exploring the movie of her life. She stopped at a time when she was a nursery school teacher. It was the end of a school day and the end of a term; the parents were coming to collect their children. Dawn, the mother of a girl in her class called Deborah, waited by the door and Margaret noticed she was upset. On speaking to her, Margaret discovered she needed to get rid of her dog, a Red Setter, because her husband had told her he would put it down. Her son Alex had been asking for a dog and his birthday was coming up. She knew that the promise to walk him would soon fade and it would fall to her to ensure he had regular exercise, but she liked the idea of regular walks on the little moor close by to keep her active. Dawn was overjoyed when Margaret suggested she might be able take the dog herself, and Margaret witnessed the physical relief in her face and shoulders as if a great burden had been lifted. This must have been a huge concern, thought Margaret. She wanted to check with the rest of her children that this was something they all wanted, so she told Dawn that she would let her know tomorrow when she dropped Deborah off in the morning. Margaret then "experienced" this situation from Dawn's point of view.

Dawn walked in the door of her flat and was met by her husband John who wasn't normally back before her, so she realised she must have been longer than she thought.

"Where the hell have you been?. You should have been home half an hour ago. I told you if you didn't get rid of the dog I would be taking him to the vets' to be put down".

"I *have* found someone to take Red, I'm taking him with me tomorrow afternoon when I collect Deborah from the nursery," Dawn protested.

"So it's all sorted, John". This wasn't exactly true but she couldn't risk letting him know it wasn't definite.

Her husband was drunk and she knew how contrary he could be, so she would have to tread carefully with him and minimize the chance of him getting worked up and potentially violent.

"I'll get the tea on. Go and play in your room Deborah, I'll give you a shout when your tea's ready". Deborah detected a tense atmosphere and obeyed immediately. She knew that protective tone and was happy to get away from her father.

Dawn had been married to John for 10 years now and the relationship had deteriorated year on year. John was an alcoholic and was a Jekyll and Hyde character. He had never hit Deborah, but he had hit Dawn many times and threatened to kill the dog. She had been planning her escape for a long time, but knew the Women's Refuge didn't take pets, and she loved Red so much she couldn't bear to leave him with the monster that her husband had become. She decided tomorrow she would persuade Margaret to take Red to give him a new life with a wonderful family. She really liked Deborah's teacher, as did her daughter. She was a very caring woman, so Dawn felt sure Red would be well looked after and probably spoilt by her children. At the weekend when her husband was away working, she would gather the necessary belongings she had secretly been storing away over the months and she'd flee the house with Deborah in the hope of getting away from John once and for all. All it would take was a phone call to a woman who worked at the Council, who had been supporting her this last year.

Margaret did take Red home the next day and he became a source of joy for the whole family. He was a beautiful dog, though he had a habit of greeting visitors by standing on his back legs and putting his paws on their shoulders, which was fine for most people but a shock for Great Aunty Wyn!

Margaret continued to follow how things played out for Dawn and Deborah, and witnessed how the simple fact of taking her dog off her hands enabled Dawn to escape from her abusive husband.

After a few months in a refuge, she and her daughter set up a new home in Scotland near friends. They thrived, and slowly built a happier and more stable life. This gave Margaret a feeling of deep joy knowing how much this had helped. She had no idea that this had happened. There had been no communication from the Council to the Nursery at the time, but it explained why little Deborah never returned for the next school year. All she knew was that they had moved to Scotland to be with family.

I think it is time we left, but now that you know of this room you can return anytime; just look for a vacant booth and you can come and go at your leisure, Margaret. Now I would like to show you something special.

Orker produced a wand. It was made of

quartz crystal and it glowed intermittently. He drew a large circle in the air and a tunnel appeared - Orker took her hand and encouraged her forward into the tunnel. It was dark but she could still see; it twisted and turned downwards. Eventually the tunnel opened out into a small dark room where a woman sat at a table at the far end. The air was heavy and she tried to move, but it was like wading through treacle. Orker was by her side and kept smiling at her. The door behind her opened, and much to her surprise her youngest daughter, Rose, walked in.

She felt emotion rise in her like an ocean surging forward, it was so wonderful to see her. Margaret followed behind Rose as she walked down the narrow room and sat on a chair opposite the woman. The woman, whom she knew was called Joan, looked up and smiled at her. Margaret instinctively put her hands on Rose's shoulders and Orker passed her a golden cross on a chain to put around her daughter's neck. Joan observed the whole thing.

"Who is Margaret?" she asked, "Your mother has just walked in behind you and put a gold cross around your neck for protection. She will always be there to look after you and keep your head above water."

Joan is a medium, Orker explained. She can see you but she can't see me, as my vibration is too fine. She is very gifted and can pass information to Rose from you if you wish her to, and Joan is also able to ask you questions. You will be able to do this on your own in time but I am here to assist

68

for the moment. What would you really like Rose to know at this time?

Joan proceeded to pass advice and guidance from Margaret to Rose about her life, and reassured her that her mother loved her deeply and would always be at her side. Margaret could see lots of colours within her daughter's body as well as some darker patches and a grey band of light around her. This concerned Margaret because she knew it was an emotional wall that Rose had built around her to protect herself from further hurt. This barrier would reduce Rose's access to her own intuition that would guide her forward in life. Rose smoked, and this also masked strong emotions, but made them easier to cope with, so for now it was necessary. She hadn't grieved properly and Margaret understood it would take time.

She started feeling exceptionally tired. Joan looked up for the last time and thanked her for coming. Margaret kissed Rose on the top of her head and wrapped her arms around her.
It's time to go and recharge but we will come back again.

In a blink they were travelling back through the tunnel and she started to feel lighter. Then they were outside the building by the pillars and she could hear the birdsong
Well done, Margaret, we have covered a lot of ground. We can visit the rest of your children later, but for now I'll take you back to your soul group so you can catch up with them and build up your energy. Just take my hand.

Nnnnnineteen

Turning nineteen was a memorable time. I moved in with three friends, Ava, Frank, and John, who were also 19 years old. Our new home was a three storey house in the West End of Newcastle that Fred, a friend of Ava's, had bought and was renting out; it was number 19. The radio resounded with the sound of [8]Paul Hardcastle's huge hit '19' so it felt appropriate to paint "Nnnnnineteen" on the front door. It was a creative den. Ava sang, Fred played sax, John acted, Frank played guitar and I did photography. We fitted easily together like a child's jigsaw, a family without parents. We were stoned most days and went out clubbing regularly, returning home to continue the party. Some people would visit and then end up moving in. A film student called Jenny arranged for our house to be used in a film and then never left after it was finished. A girl called Lucy, who was originally from Preston, visited then just stayed. Alex would stay when he was home on leave and moved in permanently when he left the Navy.

The house was a honey pot to creative bees. There was always someone new calling round and getting involved in the latest amusement. Ziggy, my cat, came with me to the house. He went missing in the first few weeks and I was beside myself with worry; where we lived wasn't the best area for cats. I hunted everywhere for him and left posters around the streets. After a week I decided to go back to my brother's flat where Ziggy had been living with me and Stevie. I didn't know what else to do.

On the second occasion I heard his "miaow", looked out the front door, and there he was, looking much thinner but otherwise well. He had travelled at least 5 miles though probably a lot further, and crossed a major road. Gratefully he never disappeared again.

**

Around this time I met and fell for a guy called Campbell. The relationship started off well enough, though there were signs and clues that I chose to ignore. He had recently finished a relationship with a nurse who would sometimes sit outside his house waiting for him. There was also another ex who would turn up from time to time, but he was adamant it was over as she was with someone else. None of this mattered until I invested a larger part of myself into the relationship and from that point forward I began losing my power. I was very lost still and hadn't begun to connect to my deep emotions. I was free to experiment with drugs and alcohol with a close-knit group of friends whose lives had been granted the same freedom for various reasons. Taking drugs together brought me a strong sense of belonging and family where there wasn't one anymore. It was a powerful draw, and an easy way to entertain yourself despite the inherent dangers, but at the time that just added to the excitement,

Campbell slowly chipped away at my

fragile confidence in subtle ways. He could change from being a critical tyrant to an effusive charmer in the blink of an eye. When friends called round they were none the wiser of the vitriol he'd spewed just minutes before their arrival. It was all easy, cheesy banter and smiles until everyone left, then he would flick back to being a twat. I don't wish to spend time on this relationship, but suffice to say I lost myself entirely in the harsh dynamics. His sadistic sleight of hand fitted perfectly into my masochistic glove. It was a pseudo- intimacy, co-dependency disguised as love, and destined to lead to a miserable place.

One night I walked back from his place after a particularly nasty character assassination over God knows what. I received an image in my mind of a pilot light deep inside the core of my being, and "heard" my mother's voice firmly saying, "He will never put your light out". Happy memories from my childhood flooded in. I'd only had 12 years of my mother's love and protection but I knew in that moment it was enough. I was not the nasty person Campbell accused me of being, and I deserved better. My insight would illuminate the way forward out of the dark, one step at a time.

Eventually I ended our relationship after a few false attempts. When giving up any bad habit, its difficult not to relapse and keep doing the same thing. It was a long road I walked to recover the part of myself I had lost. Confusion, depression, fear, anxiety and an unreachable loneliness were my companions for a number of years. My brother

Alex played an important part in freeing me from it. He was always someone I could trust completely. So when Campbell tried to make out Alex didn't have my best interests at heart, I knew he was full of shit. Alex would never try and "score points off me" as he was so fond of saying. His antics were rumbled and I was starting to understand what his game was. Alex was studying Psychology at the time, and explained that Campbell was somewhat Machiavellian, deceitful and unscrupulous. I had lots of friends and plenty to offer, so he would see me as a goody box for him to help himself to and it didn't really have anything to do with me. Finally the spell was broken, and I stopped trying to work out whether he did care about me or not because I realized I didn't even like him anymore.

***

I was working in a TexMex restaurant at the time and moved to the other side of the City to live with a friend and colleague called Candy, and her boyfriend Russ. We all worked together, and socialised after a late shift.

Candy and I had spotted each other at the initial meeting for the new staff held prior to the restaurant opening. I had that feeling of connection you have with someone who subsequently becomes an important part of your life. She was a live wire, always chatty and looking for fun. My mother would have referred to her as a flibbertigibbet as she rarely kept still.

Candy had been a nurse, so for all she was a hedonist, she was exactly the right person to help in a crisis. Candy really understood that I was trying to get out of a bad relationship. We worked on the bar together, and I wasn't eating properly and was exhausted from perpetual worry and discord with Campbell. She let me sleep under the bar, out of sight, whilst she busied herself prepping cocktails and cleaning glasses.

Unfortunately most of us were made redundant when the restaurant didn't bring in enough to justify the army of staff taken on.

Candy and Russ moved out to get a place together and Lucy from "Nnnnnineteen" moved in with me. Lucy had spiky blonde hair and was bubbly and carefree. Like Candy, she was a balm to my complex emotions. She had the confidence of someone who was used to singing and performing from a young age to an appreciative audience, which she had.

I was out of work for a few months so it was a real financial struggle. I often accompanied Lucy to the Working Men's clubs on a Sunday when she would enter the Go As You Please singing competition. My friend Andy would drive us and sometimes get to have a go on the drums. It was the cheapest night possible, and more often than not Lucy would win with her strong voice and pleasing smile.

I took an intensive typing course the Government offered for free, and eventually it would open up more employment opportunities than I could have imagined.

Maggie

Coming home on the local bus one day I was intrigued by two lasses sitting on the top deck on the other side from me. One was tall with a large, blonde hair creation, spangled with coloured ribbons. Her clothes were unique, probably handmade. The girl next to her had long, medium brown hair and was dressed in tight jeans and a leather jacket with a European look. They were having the best time, chatting on to each other, oblivious of everyone else and producing gales of laughter. I had that sense of recognition again that I already "knew" the dark haired girl.

A few weeks later I met her again as we waited to cross the road together near to my home. We got chatting and hit it off immediately. It became apparent that she lived in the street next to me. After that meeting we never lost touch. Maggie was a one-off. She was from Ayrshire in Scotland, and she spoke fast and soft with a perpetual giggle, so it was hard to understand her. I would often ask her to repeat herself, but eventually I got attuned or maybe she spoke more slowly. Either way, Maggie had a lot to say that was well worth listening to. She was the Queen Bee of The Percy, a traditional bikers' pub in town with a proper rock juke box.

Through Maggie I ended up working there with her on a Sunday night, though it didn't feel like work at all. Maggie worked on the bar upstairs where reggae was played, and I stayed downstairs with the rock music and the bikers, lining up their bike helmets behind the bar. Drinking and smoking behind the bar was expected. After our shift we would head out to an underground blues party in some house over in the West End of Newcastle, the whereabouts of which Maggie had previously established, a hideaway to relax to big Reggae sounds, share a smoke and indulge in some home-cooked Caribbean food.

Maggie had moments of searing insight sourced, no doubt, from her Celtic roots. I was out with her one night at a place called the Jewish Mother. I was sitting on a bar stool with a can of Red Stripe in my hand. She stated that something or someone was covering my light. She knew very little about me because we just played in the moment and didn't discuss the past much, but clearly saw through my mask. Unsure of everything, I found it hard to make decisions or trust many people, but I trusted Maggie and it suited me fine to hold on to her leather biker jacket and let it whisk me to new places and people, surrounded by good music. She was a real tonic and I trusted her. Maggie was at a crossroads herself. She was finishing a Communications degree and wasn't sure what to do or whether to stay in Newcastle. I was finding Newcastle too small as I'd bumped into Campbell too many times already. I knew I had to leave Newcastle.

My sister lived in Weymouth in Dorset and I arranged to move down to live with her and her boyfriend. Lucy was happy to move in with Candy, so it all worked out well. Maggie was one of my closest friends then and it was hard to leave her, but she was very supportive and said she was impressed by my courage. She even gave me the amazing jeans she was wearing when I first saw her that time on the bus. I knew she would come and visit me because she couldn't resist an adventure, and she did.

Alex kindly took my beloved Ziggy in to join his lovely ginger and white cat Bob. After a few months in sunny Weymouth, circumstances at Ruth's work led Ruth and I to move to London which was where I really wanted to be, as my friends Ava, Jenny and Frank were already there. The anonymity was delicious. I could build my shattered confidence and reinvent myself.

***

I once read that London is a Gemini sign, quick moving and thinking, communicative, and sociable. Living there at that time was the perfect prescription. It felt safe and vibrant. The music industry was still controlled by record companies, and that's where I wanted to work. I temped for a number of them, but settled with Arista in their Marketing Department. I adored it and got on well with everyone. However, there was always a chance your face wouldn't fit any more and you would be replaced. Some people ended up working there based on who they knew and not what they could do, but they didn't usually last; it was necessary to deliver. I was a grafter and would rise to any challenge no matter how quirky.

I'd arrive about 10 am and work constantly

all day, smoking at my desk and drinking pop, rushing out to McDonalds to grab a McChicken burger and a can of Sprite. Around 5.20 pm I would help myself to a can of Budweiser from the fridge and head home about 6 pm, unless there was an Arista band to go and support. One morning I walked in the office to see my colleague Chris on the office floor simulating sex with a full length poster of Barry Manilow, which had just arrived hot off the press, the whole department standing round in amusement. Chris was a really great guy and Barry was one of his artists. I worked closely with him and took frequent calls from Barry's fans. They were beyond passionate and had to be taken very seriously. Chris was a Londoner; he had a kind heart and a great sense of humour. I learned a lot from him about how important it was to make phone calls a pleasure. He was everyone's friend and a great communicator, and people enjoyed working with him.

He brought Barry Manilow upstairs when he visited so I could meet him too. Being a temp I wasn't invited to the team meeting so that was typically thoughtful of Chris. Manilow was very charismatic, and so well groomed he glowed. After looking around our office he made the following remark,

"Jeez there's such a lot of crap in here!".

Which to be fair was true, as the office held the majority of stock and promotional materials on all the artists.

Record companies at the time relied on Radio One DJs to promote their artists by getting them onto their play lists. New gimmicks were dreamed up all the time; dancing flowers and giant umbrellas. I was tasked with finding a confectioner in London who could spin a chocolate egg around a CD single for the latest Carly Simon release.

I was in the office when a new girl appeared at the fax machine which was near my desk. The conversation went something like this;

"Hello, I don't think we've met, I'm Rose, who are you?" I offered.

"My name's Isla I work in PR", she responded.

"Which part of Scotland are you from?" I asked detecting her accent.

"Livingston, West Lothian. Where are you from?".

"I'm from Newcastle. I've been to Livingston a few times, my mother has a close friend who lives there. Which part of London do you live in?"

"Earlsfield, near Wimbledon. I'm here with my partner Craig".

"Oh I live in Wimbledon Park with my sister, so we're very near you".

We established that we literally lived down the road from each other, quite a coincidence given the size of London. That first meeting was the start of a lifelong friendship, and we spent many occasions in each other's homes.

***

Isla and Craig were an attractive couple. Craig had long wavy blonde hair which he tossed back when he laughed, which was often. Isla was slim with long dark hair and piercing blue eyes, the picture of Celtic beauty. They had seen just about every rock band there was to see, and they dressed the part.

It suited me working in a creative environment with colourful characters, but I yearned for some answers. I had lost myself in the toxic relationship I'd left behind in Newcastle, and I needed to understand how it had happened so it couldn't happen again. I was only interested in having friendships with men as it all felt too scary.

I started reading books on the metaphysical, and often visited a bookshop near Charing Cross called 'Mysteries'. The books opened my mind and I became increasingly sensitive. I had a dream about my mother and it felt real. I used to dream that she was walking along the street where we lived, and then I'd be hit by the awful truth that she wasn't here any more. This dream was different. I met her on a beach, and she passed important information to me and I felt her deep love for me. I woke up exhilarated but with a peculiar feeling that lingered all day, like I was trapped inside a "heavy body" and the dream world was the real world.

London began to feel unsafe and I longed for a kinder environment. I was fed up with seeing commuters pushing on and off trains shoving smaller, older people out of the way. There were no dogs anywhere, other than Ruth's beautiful

Poppy who was a chocolate Field Spaniel. When we took her on the tube people visibly melted, discarding their stern expressions. I had a foreboding of a train disaster and I also dreamt of a passenger plane crash that killed many people.

On the morning of 12 December 1988, my sister and I were heading to work. We waited on the train platform at Surbiton for the next Waterloo train. It arrived as usual and Ruth got on. I followed behind her and went to step on but my court shoe fell off between the platform and the train and onto the track. I would have to wait for the train to move out before I could get it. I told Ruth to stay on and I'd see her later tonight after work, but she insisted on waiting with me.

The next train we boarded stopped just outside of Wimbledon. We were left without an explanation for some time. Internet and mobiles didn't exist so all the passengers were in the dark together.

Eventually there came an announcement that the train wouldn't be going any further because there had been an incident further along the track, and we were asked to leave the train immediately.

We decided to explore Wimbledon as we were looking for alternative accommodation because our brother Robert and his wife would be returning to their flat in Surbiton, where we were currently staying. At lunchtime we went to a pub, and it was there that we heard there had been a terrible train crash outside of Clapham Junction, which was the original train we would have got if my shoe hadn't come off. That day 35 people were killed and 484 were injured. It was sobering news and we were bewildered by the incident with my shoe.

As it happened, we ended up moving to Wimbledon Park after finding a great flat at the top of a large, old house up from the tube station. I became increasingly nervous about travelling around London. I was never very keen on the underground train and I just became worn out from the constant travelling. I wasn't successful in applying for a permanent job at Arista and thought it must be time to move on, so instead I took a long term temping job at an engineering company in Wimbledon.

A friend from Newcastle called Keith moved in with Ruth and me for a short period when he was stuck for somewhere to live. My sister was in the process of extricating herself from the Royal Navy; she needed to be free to be herself and wanted to get a mobile home and travel around the UK. She eventually left and moved back to Weymouth to stay with her boyfriend. Keith moved out, and Ava and her boyfriend, who were between places, moved in with me. It was becoming clear that my time in London was coming to an end. I was ready for a change and didn't want to stay in London on my own. I was interested in Brighton or Edinburgh, but then I had a dream that I was walking into a flat in my hometown Newcastle and it felt fantastic and right. I didn't make the decision based solely on the dream, but it certainly put the option on the table and it's what I chose. Ava kept the place on and Keith, who was originally from Newcastle, kindly drove me back up with my belongings. I moved in temporarily with friends and then Alex, and eventually got my own place.

Isla and Craig remained in London but returned to Livingston a year or so later, but we kept in touch.

Rainbows

Margaret had been in Heaven for several Earth years by now. She had remembered so much since returning, including how time itself operated differently. The past, present and future could all be accessed at any moment, and each year on Earth was like the length of a DVD which she could rewind and forward to enter her children's lives. She could be with all four of them at the same time, but significant energy and preparation were required to accomplish that.

She had chosen to work with children again as she had on Earth. This time she "nursed" the souls of children who had died through tragic circumstances, and offered intensive care and healing to help them adjust to their new environment and erase dark memories of their death. She worked in a "hospital", but it was very different from anything she had worked in on Earth. Margaret's particular gifts were compassion and a deeply grounded love that held no judgement. It rendered her able to receive souls who had been distraught through the trauma of horrific accidents, illness, torture and murder.

Angels dedicated to working in this field were assigned to the trauma situation prior to death, and would assist the soul to arrive in Heaven. They would transmit the circumstances of each death to a panel of highly evolved souls and then on to Margaret and her team, an angelic triage, so they could allocate the "nurse" who could best care for and reawaken the newly arrived soul. The hospital itself was a wondrous place. It had no ceiling, so the sky would alter constantly, offering golden sunshine and gorgeous sunsets depending on the emotional needs of those in the building at any one time. It was a great joy to work in this area because she could affect such transformation for every soul.

There were treatment rooms dedicated to different colours of the rainbow, as well as rooms that immersed souls in every colour simultaneously. Light was used constantly to heal jagged emotional states and imbue peace and calm once again. Some rooms were lined with walls of crystals that undulated as they cleansed the atmosphere of negativity. Ambient music was constantly played in the background. Music and singing played a major role in healing, but also in celebrations as well.

As well as choosing to work here, Margaret enjoyed a variety of activities away from the hospital. She spent a lot of time with her soul group. Sometimes they would go on a picnic in the countryside, where they would encounter animals from all over the world living peacefully alongside each other. She was allergic to horses on Earth, but here she could spend hours with them, riding in whatever terrain she fancied at the time. She was able to communicate with the horses so they would negotiate with her where they wished to go.

Orker continued to meet up with her when she had a task to complete that would connect her back to Earth. He would appear like the shop assistant from "[9]Mr Benn", the popular children's programme in the seventies, and she would know that someone somewhere on Earth required her assistance. Inevitably it was one of her children or grandchildren and sometimes other family members or friends.

***

Margaret was reading a book and relaxing at her home when Orker appeared in front of her.

Your daughters are close to danger but it can be avoided. We need to go to the Transformation Tower.

The tower was a large ancient looking building, a bit like the tower of Pisa but dead straight. Inside, it was technology gone mad. Fluid-like screens surrounded the rounded walls on each floor, of which there were at least 100. Orker settled them at a particular screen. He waved his hand in front of it and revealed the scene of a train crash on Earth. There was a date and time counter flicking away in the top right corner. He rewound the events back to earlier in the day and froze it at a scene where her two daughters were standing waiting on a train station platform in Southern England.

In order to ensure their safety, I need you to imagine both your daughters bound together by strong, thick golden chords that wrap around them both and keep them connected. Meanwhile I am going to concentrate on knocking a shoe from your daughter Rose as she steps onto the oncoming train, and prevent them from boarding it.

They began the energy work, and as they did so a curtain of purple light drew around them to afford some privacy from the other screens where many other souls were working. Margaret found it easy to concentrate. She recalled memories of the two girls playing closely together when they were younger, as she knew this would strengthen their bond. Orker was quietly fixated on the screen and the task in hand. After a short while the curtain dissolved and the atmosphere changed and became lighter. Margaret let out a huge yawn. Orker pressed the button to play the scene out. They watched as both girls remained on the platform as the train left the station, and avoided the imminent crash. There was palpable relief from Margaret, but she needed to know more about the crash and looked into Orker's eyes for some answers.

Disasters are inevitable and there is nothing that could have stopped this one, though many more people could have died or been injured without the intervention of protection as we have just given. It wasn't for your daughters to experience and it certainly wasn't their time to die. As your understanding of energy grows, you will be able to orchestrate many types of protection and guidance so that you can continue to ensure the safety of your family and friends in many wonderful ways.

Margaret had acquired quite a lot of experience since her arrival. She regularly visited Earth to be with her beloved children. She would find a tranquil place to sit, close her eyes and ask to be connected to whoever she wanted to be with. She wouldn't always see the person clearly, as it would depend on their emotional and physical state and what they were doing, but often she could stay close and walk with them to offer some telepathic guidance or to pass on a feeling of love and comfort. The act of being near someone would automatically raise their vibrational frequency which could help to pull someone out of a negative feeling.

Alternatively she would feel an emotional pull and see an image of the person who was thinking about her and wanting to speak with her. This exercise was relatively easy for her now that she had recovered fully from her own illness and grief since passing over. Sometimes she would send a rainbow to her children when they were struggling with a situation that was bringing them despair. The colours represented all the different people in the world and how, in reality, we are all connected; it is a powerful symbol of harmony and hope. Many souls choose to reach their loved ones through meteorological communication.

A special building was designated for this purpose. Rainbows could be conjured up on demand. Names of people on Earth were passed to specially trained souls who would spin golden threads of light to each person, weaving them into a rainbow manifestation, conjured up in a group meditation which Margaret would join. The meditation room was spherical and the size of a house. Weather was projected on to the translucent walls, reflecting the focus of their meditation, which in this case was a rainbow, but could be any other meteorological event. The chosen people will be drawn energetically to where they can observe the rainbow and link to their sender and pick up their message of hope. If the desire of the meditation group is strong enough, it could appear even when there is no sunshine.

Another "trick" she was taught was to exude an aroma around her children to reassure them of her close presence. Margaret loved the scent of freesias so chose this as her calling card. However it is in dreams where she was particularly free to connect with her children.

Heaven Scent

I couldn't have left Newcastle if Alex hadn't taken in my beloved cat, Ziggy, and as soon as I got my own place he moved back in with me. Ziggy became a large tabby; he had huge, round eyes which he used to discern my visitors. He loved to lie full length along my back when I was reading a book. I was very close to him, and having been single for a few years it was me and him all the way. I used to worry about leaving him because I lived in a rough part of Newcastle and there were horror stories of cats being stolen for dog fights.

One night I was out with my party animal friend Lorrie and we went back to her place, which was at the top of my street. We were there until the early hours, just drinking and smoking and having a laugh. I started getting a strange headache and it wasn't a normal one. I had images of Ziggy flashing into my head, so I was really worried. I told everyone that I was worried that something had happened to my cat and said I'd have to go home. A nice guy called Mike offered to come with me, as it was now about 3 am in the morning.

He walked me to my door then was about to head off, but I asked him to hang on. I went towards my door and it just swung open. My heart sank and adrenalin kicked in; someone had been in. I rushed in, looking for Ziggy. He wasn't visible, and I started to panic, running from room to room. Eventually, he gingerly appeared, he'd been hiding, but he was alright just really spooked.

It was only after finding Ziggy safe that I could take in I'd been burgled. My belongings were scattered around and my CD collection and ghetto blaster had gone. I couldn't believe it. In some ways I was more stunned that I'd picked up a message from my beloved cat. I rang the Police and waited for them to arrive, having straightened up immediately. After they left I secured the house and took Ziggy with me to stay at Lorrie's for the night. Alex still lived down the road, and the next day he fixed a new lock on the front door. I was immensely grateful and relieved, though I'd never feel the same again about living there.

***

I had various jobs over the next few years after temping for a while, and ended up working as Production Secretary for a children's TV programme. It was very different from working in the music industry, less cool and more "dahling". The women seemed to be much stronger characters than the men, and it was very cliquey. I didn't fit in, I was too real. My favourite people were the carpenters, finance team and the sound man, but then sound men are always sound. I used to escape to the mobile Sound unit whenever possible. The guy I worked for clearly had issues, including unrequited love for one of the female writers.

I wasn't happy there but didn't know what else I could do. One day I was in the office feeling particularly lonely and despondent, whilst everyone talked about themselves. I recall smelling an aroma around me that was so strong I was trying to locate its source. It was the sublime scent of Freesias and made me think of my mother. She loved them, and when my sister and I laid flowers for her at a private memorial service, I chose Freesias. So I have always associated them with her. It was very comforting amidst the isolation of the office. I couldn't visualise a future there, but didn't know what to do as it was good pay and I lived alone with my cat Ziggy, and had to support myself.

I was still working there when I woke up one morning and found Ziggy lying on his side by the edge of the room, struggling to breathe. I was beside myself. I rang in sick and got him up to the local vet. I had very little spare cash but agreed to an operation that might help him.

On returning to work, I was asked to go and see the boss in his office immediately. When I got there, Anita from Finance was already seated and glanced at me apprehensively. The Director of the programme blurted out that I was no longer required and he wanted me to leave immediately. My mind was spinning; part of me was elated at the prospect of leaving, but another part was wondering how I would financially survive. There was no explanation, so I pushed for one and received a pathetic excuse. Previous secretaries had pandered to his neurotic personality and I'd done none of it, so I knew it had everything to do with that. Anita kindly drove me home and stayed for a cup of tea and a chat to check I was okay.

She told me not to give it any thought but to move on, and that she had insisted he pay me a bit more as it was just before Christmas. It was a shock but also a great relief not to have to go there any more, plus I had a few thousand pounds in the bank so could easily pay any vet bills now.

Ziggy recovered from the operation, but sadly they discovered a hole in his diaphragm which they said could have resulted from having a shock. I thought of the burglary and felt terrible. They also said he had feline AIDS so things weren't looking good. Sadly I had no option other than to put my beloved companion to "sleep". I was devastated and I felt I'd let him down. He was only 9 years old.

It was only after Ziggy died that I realised how protected I'd felt by him. I relied on him to let me know if there was anyone around, especially at night. I was heartbroken at losing him and full of guilt for putting him to sleep. I was inconsolable; no-one could understand what he had meant to me, though some tried to say helpful things. Ziggy was a wise cat. If he didn't like someone he certainly let them know. He would turn his back on them or just sit and stare at them from a distance with his huge saucer eyes. He was my guardian and now I was all alone. At least I didn't have to face going to work and could take time out to grieve for Ziggy. I wondered about the scent of Freesias I had smelled at work. I wondered if my mother was trying to let me know she was around,

Within a week I had an unusual dream. I

woke up in the middle of the night, but the bedroom was in grey light. I sat up in bed and looked around. I could see everything clear as crystal, even though it was "dark". There were clothes on the back of a chair which I could make out in great detail. All of a sudden there was a bright flash and a loud crack in front of me, then Ziggy appeared from thin air and dropped on to my lap. He looked so healthy and fluffy, not how he had appeared when I last saw him at the vet's. I stroked him and told him I loved him, it was wonderful. When I woke in the morning I recalled the "dream". I felt emotional and elated, my guilt had vanished and my grief had subsided, it was amazing. I was convinced the experience was real and was so grateful for it, as it helped me to forgive myself and move forward, and I knew I had to move.

***

I found a flat over on the East side of Newcastle sharing with a stranger who turned out to be a very peculiar and damaged woman, so I moved again, this time into a lovely big house with two guys who I met through my friend Cerys.

Cerys was an amazing woman who I vaguely knew socially. However, when my temping job sent me to her office situated in an Adult Education Centre, we got to know each other well. Cerys was a powerhouse of intelligence and sensitivity, fuelled with a disarming humour often to the detriment of herself.

She was committed to improving people's lives and worked smartly and it appeared effortlessly, whisking out life changing reports and strategies, yet often heading home with a forgotten pen protruding from her thick, dark hair, piled up in a *laissez faire* style. Cerys opened up a whole new world for me where success, ambition and hilarious fun were all possibilities. I felt appreciated and looked after. At first, my self esteem was so low I was unsure of what I had to offer in return, but Cerys could see who I really was. She had a magical way of saying and doing the right thing, and always with absolute modesty.

Along with Alex, she was instrumental in helping me maintain the confidence to stay away from Campbell, who never really ended his relationships but sought to manipulate his way back in when it suited.

In time I met a guy called Fraser and moved in with him. It was an important transitional relationship after the turbulence of Campbell. He was calm and easygoing, and we had some fun but it wasn't lighting up all the boxes. After a year and a bit it ended, I moved out and rented a bed sit from a friend who lived with parrots. It was perfect for the short term, but then I was ready for my own place and another cat. Eventually I settled in a tiny flat in Jesmond, in a small block owned by a Housing Association.

My friend Juliet from college had a cat that had just had kittens, and she had offered one to me. The other kittens were already allocated, so I was allocated the runt of the litter, a timid female silver tabby. I visited her a number of times, and she was often hiding in her partner's cardigan pocket. When I went to collect her I was told that the person who was supposed to take one of her brothers had decided she didn't want to, and asked if I wanted both of them. Finances still weren't great, so I stood there in a dilemma trying to decide if I could afford to. Meanwhile the tiny male silver tabby kitten strutted across the room, sat at my feet and looked up imploringly. The decision was made, I had to take him. I christened them Bonny and Bruno; they were my "Bambinis" and I fell completely and utterly in love with them.

***

My Aunty Janet was ill with bone cancer at this time, and after reading a book by Betty Shine, a renowned healer, I wrote to her to ask for Janet to be sent healing. I received a letter saying she would include her on her list, and she also encouraged me to "plug" into a healing network that took place at a particular time each night. I had been informed through the family grapevine that Janet might not last beyond 2 years. Sometime after receiving the letter from Betty Shine, I "heard" the words "two months" in my head. I felt strongly that this was to encourage me to visit her sooner rather than later.

I rang my Dad to try and share my sense of urgency without going into the detail of how I knew. My stepmother answered as usual, so I tried my best to pass on the information so my Dad could visit his sister again if he wished to. However, my stepmother knew better, she had spoken with the doctors, and dismissed my comment that she may only have 2 months not 2 years to live. I couldn't be bothered to argue, but at least I had a clear conscience. The kittens were very young, but I had no choice but to leave them and get on a coach and visit my Aunty to say goodbye. A friend kindly offered to call in on them, as it would only be for one night. All went to plan and it was great to see Aunty Janet and very much herself still. Sadly, in two months she was no longer with us.

In the same block where I lived was a woman called Jean. I'd met her briefly the day I moved in and I had that strange but now familiar feeling that I was going to know her very well. She was having a drink with a girlfriend whilst looking out for their taxi to take them out for the night. You could wait in the lobby by the postbox lockers, having a glass of wine, whilst looking our for the taxi through the window. When the taxi arrived you could lock your glass in your postbox and collect it in the morning. The next time I saw Jean she was coming past my door to use the laundry. The kittens were running up and down the corridor between the two fire doors outside my front door. She adored them, and an instant connection was made between all four of us. Things just went from there. Jean lived above me, two flats away. She kindly looked after the kittens when I went to France for a wedding, otherwise I couldn't have gone.

We met up regularly as we were both really skint and so made our own entertainment. We started doing tarot card readings for each other and found we were very good. We were both single for a long time, then met our future partners within days of each other. Of course we saw it all in the cards but we didn't really believe it would happen, but it did. However, before we met them, I'd heard about a lady in Jesmond called Pauline, who gave amazing readings and I wanted to see her. I was working at the local Arts Administration, and really struggling with my boss, who was an arrogant bully. In fact the place had more than one bully, and at times I was caught between them which was becoming untenable. The organisation had some serious issues behind its glittering reputation, and there were many employees suffering as a consequence. A lot of women worked there, but it was a patriarchal set- up with a capital "P".

***

Pauline looked like an angel with glistening blonde hair, and kind blue eyes, and she turned out to be phenomenal. Her guide was a man called Alan, which I thought was great, clearly not a Native American Indian Chief on this occasion!

She used virtual scrabble to spell out names. Alan would "give" her a specific number of letters that were an anagram of a name. She gave me eight letters as follows, RGTMRAER, and I quickly worked out it was MARGARET.

We deciphered other names that were pertinent. A friend of mine went to see her later and she was given the letters that made up the name PUSHKA, her deceased Indian mother, and she was blown away, as it was not a name that would mean much to most people.

Pauline told me I would meet my soulmate before the end of the year, which seemed highly unlikely as it was already October (1998).

In December that year I did meet my soul mate; he was called Dean. When I was seventeen, I went to see his band many times with a group of mutual friends who were diehard fans. We had loads of mutual acquaintances and had crossed each other's paths constantly over the years, but as with all relationships timing is everything. We had met up briefly a few years earlier, but I wasn't ready to let anyone in and there were complications, including a young son. That last time I saw him he walked me home from our friend's house and came in for a smoke and a bacon sandwich. Before he left, later that night, I lent him a huge, warm jumper that was really long, and couldn't stop smiling as I watched him walk unpretentiously up the street with a jumper down to his knees, and the snow falling around him. In fact every time I saw him he made me laugh and smile.

Anyway, that December his band Christmas night collided with my photography class Christmas night, at the same venue, heralding that the time was right for us to come together. Dean made a grand gesture and walked across a large table laden with food so he could to talk to me. As we caught up with each other, I remember thinking how comfortable his arm felt around my waist like it was meant to be there. However, I had to flee as I had work the next day and I didn't want to give my difficult boss any ammunition to shoot at me. I really wanted to stay, but the tequila had started to flow and I knew I wouldn't make it to work if I stayed.

After that night we never stopped bumping into each other, whether it was on my way to work or shopping at the supermarket. Our baskets literally clashed coming round the corner of an aisle. I was impressed when I spied a couple of carrots, an onion and a potato in his basket. I thought this guy looks after himself and cooks from scratch.

It was now two years since I had lent Dean my jumper, and he called round to return it. He stated he had moths and was worried they were going to eat it, so he'd thought he better bring it back. Whether it was true or not, and I think it was, it made me laugh, and from then on I don't remember him not being in my life.

I had my beautiful cats and he had a dog called Rosa, AKA Rosie, AKA Rosie Malosie. She was a small black and white Collie with some Spaniel in her genes that made her bottom wiggle. She was devoted to Dean and very intelligent. I was nervous about us living together, in case the animals didn't get on, but in just over a year we all moved into a new place and became a very happy family.

***

The next ten years were occupied by my new relationship with Dean, enjoying getting to know each other, looking after all the fur babies and his young son. We didn't have much money, but we enjoyed ourselves regardless. Dean was in a rock band which I was happy to support where I could, as I was no stranger to the music scene. The weakest link in my life was work. I managed to leave the job working with the asshole, and was now working with some great people in a health setting.

One guy in particular called Connor, was a real change agent, and taught me that to influence an organisation you had to work from the inside out and challenge the "enemy" in a positive way. He was highly respected within local communities across the board, and had a great sense of humour. My knowledge and confidence grew massively from working with Connor, who gently pushed me beyond my restrictive administrative role. He was a mentor and a friend, but sadly after a couple of years he and his family returned to Ireland. When the project ended, I took on a new role promoting Fairtrade throughout Newcastle. It was a minimal role, but I picked up the baton and totally ran with it and became the North East representative, so I would visit London on a regular basis and occasionally went abroad.

The people I worked with who supported Fairtrade were passionate and driven.

Organisations I worked with shared a common aim to improve the lives of poor farmers around the world.

In 2005 I attended an International Conference in Lyon. I was very good at my job and I enjoyed it to a degree, but had little support from management at my work base. I gradually took on more and more whilst continuing to work in total isolation, as I was based in a team that had nothing to do with my work, and, other than the two young admin girls I didn't relate to any of them. I was a square peg in a round hole once again. I had started to suffer from anxiety, which meant a trip abroad entailed facing a number of worries, starting with the flight itself.

Anxiety is a silent killer. It can slowly close off all avenues of joy because everything just becomes an ordeal. It is hugely common in the world though apparently not so much amongst farmers, according to my friend who is an acupuncturist who provided treatment to farmers in Northumberland as part of a project!

The nature of anxiety means it is not something you want to admit to and share, yet in doing so there can be instant relief, which is why I wish to talk about it to say to anyone who is experiencing anxiety in any of its forms, don't keep it to yourself, and don't believe the lies it tells you about yourself and your life; it's false fear.

I was really scared of flying on my own. A few days before leaving I had a cup of tea with my old friend Frank, who I'd lived with in Benwell. He was no stranger to anxiety, his life had been a roller coaster too. We discovered that we were on exactly the same flight from Newcastle to Amsterdam and then he was going on to Miami and I was going in to France. The wonderful thing about coincidence is, it makes me feel I am in the right place at the right time, which is very reassuring. I decided I wasn't going to die on this particular flight.

I managed to attend the conference, for the 3 or 4 days I was there relying on diazepam to relieve the worst symptoms. Taking time out in the evening with the young woman called June, who I'd travelled with, I sensed she also needed to just get away for a quiet meal nearby. So it suited us both.

On the flight home I was sitting alone. June had been allocated a priority seat. I was very nervous about flying; I felt trapped with my own fears and there was no-one I could speak to. I put on my headphones and listened to "[10]In Rainbows" by Radiohead. I had a seat by the window, and as the sounds filled my head I gazed out at the clouds which were vast and ethereal. The sun threw shafts of sunlight across the scene, and a huge circular rainbow appeared in the centre. I'd never seen anything so remarkable. For the whole journey I was blissed out by the marriage of music and nature, and all my anxiety dissipated. I thought of my mother, and wondered if I was just that little bit closer to her up there in the sky. The rainbow vision totally changed my state of mind.

At that time I lost my beloved male cat, Bruno, who was only 8 years. This accounted for some of the anxiety, as I wasn't good at loss and found it life- threatening. He had kidney stones which led to kidney failure, which I understand tom cats are susceptible to. I tried everything, special food and eventually an operation to have them removed, but it was too late; the damage was done. I felt dreadful that I couldn't help him to recover. He was my "Gorgeous boy" and I was going to miss him terribly. After he had gone, I removed his bed which was under our bed and found a big white feather in it which appeared to have come from thin air. I've since experienced many white feathers appearing at times of difficulty. On one occasion, they appeared constantly on a 5 hour walk in the countryside.

***

It took me a number of years to understand the causes of my anxiety and how to diminish it and not perpetuate it. Suffice to say, it often strikes people who are sensitive, caring, considerate to the degree that they often put everyone else's needs ahead of their own. They can be perfectionists, highly creative and intelligent. If you can relate to this and are suffering from anxiety, please know that it won't last forever and can be resolved. Be selfish and put your needs first; if you aren't okay then you aren't able to help all the people you care for. Lower the bar regarding your expectations of yourself, stop trying to be perfect and just be good enough. Please don't beat yourself up, this can manifest quite literally through accidents and bumps; be gentle with yourself. Speak to someone and seek professional help if it won't go away.

Anxiety often strikes about 9 months after an initial trauma, but this can vary. We have incredible capacity to cope with difficult experiences, but it will come out later when it is "safe" to deal with the emotions. I have only experienced depression once when I was 19. It took time to resolve, but I am happy to be a member of the club for people who have been to the dark side and back. It means I can help people to recognise the symptoms and seek support. One of the great things about mental health difficulties is how it opens your mind looking for solutions. If you find practices that work, you don't care how weird they are or whether they have passed the Government's Health Select Committee or not.

I started experimenting with prayer, from a non-religious point of view. I lost my flexi card on my way to work. I was late and running to the bus stop when my white, plastic, flexi card dropped from my pocket. I stopped to pick it up but couldn't see it anywhere. I couldn't be late that day as I had an important meeting in the morning. I'd been reading a book by Doreen Virtue, which described how to find things by putting out a prayer and asking God, Universe, Source (whatever you wish to use) to look for the lost item across all time and space and bring it back to me. I decided to have a go, as prayers could be used for the most ordinary of situations.

I said the words in my head, and immediately the sun peeped out from a dark grey sky. It shone down a shaft of sunlight, and I saw something glinting like gold underneath one of the numerous parked cars. I moved towards it and got down and looked under the car, and there on the ground, only just in reach was my flexi card. It felt magical and I was taken aback. It may seem trivial but it felt like an immediate and true response to my prayer. There is no way I would have seen it if the sun hadn't come out for those brief seconds; it had bounced right underneath the car. I was intrigued and encouraged to practise more.

The next day Dean and I went swimming at our local pool. Dean was driving us out of the car park to leave. I spotted a young Boxer dog being chased by its owner. It was running recklessly around the car park and heading to the exit which led onto a main road. Dean stopped the car and I prayed for help to rescue the dog and save it from harm. We watched the Boxer race towards us from behind, and then stop abruptly right next to our car. His lead had jammed under one of our wheels and was holding him fast. The owner caught up to us and grabbed the lead and his dog. Again, it was an amazing response to my request for help, and not an action we could possibly have orchestrated ourselves.

I now use prayer all the time for people, animals, events, however small or large, from organising a special celebration to trying to get the lid off a jar!. It is of no consequence how small the request other than the positive intention. I can't comment on praying with a harmful intention as

I've never done it, but the school of thought is that whatever you send out will come back to you threefold, so it would be a dangerous exercise to engage in. Results are always positive and sometimes miraculous, but it is important to let go of wanting to control the outcome, as things are often better than I can possibly imagine. In terms of protecting animals or people at immediate risk, I have honed my prayer into one word for speed; "protect". I've used it frequently for animals crossing busy roads and I have never seen anything come to harm yet.

Tidal Wave

Full to the Brim
(By Author Monday 14 November 2011)

The floodgates are locked
I don't have the key
The water rises up in me
Tea and sympathy, coffee and beer
Ready to listen but nothing to hear.

Magical moments glint in my mind
Slow motion images smiling and kind
Treasured conversations hang in the air
Choking my heart with rising despair
Vacuous faces offer no balm
Maybe it's the storm before the calm.

Halleluiah My Sweet Lord
The cast is changing, who will applaud
Multiple choices beckon ahead
The path of least resistance is the road I tread.

Dust yourself off, forage for your dreams

Gorge on your future, burst at the seams

Fly over mountains

Sail across seas

Dance in the starlight

Follow the bees

Blurt the unspeakable

Topple the top

Scream from the inside

Maybe you'll stop.

Into tranquillity

Soak up the peace

Know in your soul

The darkness will cease.

There comes a point in life when you look back over your photographs and realise that many of the people and pets in them aren't here anymore. It's a salient moment. We wish we had seen them more often and given them more of ourselves, regretting those occasions we were irritated by them, the disagreements we invested our energy in, and how ashamedly trivial they were in retrospect.

In October my brother Robert was seriously ill in hospital following an operation to remove a large part of his liver. It was a precaution, as remarkably he had fought 3 types of cancer already so there was a concern it had returned. It was a serious operation and recovery was always going to have risks. He was left hanging by a thread as he wrestled with kidney failure that didn't seem to be responding to treatment. I travelled down to visit him at the intensive care unit. My journey down to Guildford Hospital was weird. I felt utterly protected; it's hard to describe. My emotions felt calmed and directed somehow. I dislike the London tube when it's packed, but I knew I had to brave it if I was to make my train connection from Waterloo to Guildford. I felt I was in a bubble of protection and nothing could upset me.

The tube journey was fine and I headed on to Guildford and Robert's bedside. He was very ill with poor liver and kidney function. The opiates he was being administered were giving him hallucinations, He told me the people from Auschwitz wondering around were worrying him, so I told him just to ignore them as they wouldn't harm him. He then told an incredible story to me and the nurse about an important person who had visited the hospital last night, wanting to close it down. Robert had been arguing on behalf of the hospital to keep it open but he needed our help with the situation as it was serious. It was great to be physically with him as he had been in an induced coma for a while, prior to my arrival. It was the next day, after visiting him and preparing to say goodbye that I was really nervous, because I knew I would have a strong sense of whether I would see him again or not. As it happened I felt good and didn't feel upset so this was a great sign. I headed back up to Newcastle with what I coin Post Traumatic Joy Syndrome (PTJS).

Shortly after my visit I had a dream where the words BENIGN appeared horizontally and repeatedly across his body, and I was reassured by this and told his wife. She later contacted me to let me know the lump was benign and Robert slowly made an incredible recovery. He returned to the hospital months later to thank the staff for their care, and told me they didn't know who he was at first because they really hadn't expected him to survive. It was a massive relief for everyone.

***

Our beautiful dog Rosa was always bursting with energy, wired for activity. It was impossible for us to imagine her getting old, but aged around 15 or so she started to show signs of slowing down. She went steadily downhill over a period of a just a few months. Close friends lost their dogs in succession, Bruce an Australian Cattle Dog and Harry, Rosa's boyfriend, a Jack Russell, and I *knew* Rosa would be number three because I could sense the inherent warning of a third loss to come.

On 21st December 2010 we put Rosa to sleep and were utterly devastated. It was so hard to see people with their dogs or listen to people talking about them. Not everyone understands the heart break of losing a cherished pet.

"Why don't you get another one?" people suggest. You wouldn't say that about a member of your family.

"Sorry to hear your Grandma has died, why don't you get another one?"
Rosa left a huge hole in our lives, for a couple of months our daily life had revolved around her every need.

Snow came early that year, and on Christmas morning we headed down to the field at the bottom of our street, an automatic reflex kicking in, to take Rosa out for her first walk of the day. Our heads and hearts hung heavy as we crunched across the white blanket without her. There wasn't a soul about. No doubt presents were being ripped open and large turkey' manoeuvered into small ovens.

Across the field in the distance a man appeared with his black and white Collie. In the next moment, the dog came charging over to Dean first and then me, jumping up at us to say hello. The man came running over, apologising profusely that his dog had never done that before. We tried to explain that it was more than okay, but we didn't want to explain why, as this would take the lid off our raw emotions and we weren't sure what would come out. It was a drop of balm in our grief for Rosie. It has happened since many times with Rosa's Sheepdog cousins. Does she send them to us or do they just know we need a connection to her? One time on holiday in Wales, we were walking in the countryside around Powys and a farmer had his dog riding up with him on his noisy red tractor. The sheepdog jumped off and ran over to us, which was some distance, passed on Rosa's greeting and then headed back to her Master's side, much to his bewilderment.

Bonny was our remaining pet, so she was very precious to us. Dean was totally bereft without his adoring Rosa who had seen him through so much and had been his loyal and affectionate companion. I sent Rosa's picture to an animal communicator in a national magazine, and she wrote back asking if she could put her on the front page and feature her in her column. I also sent a photo of Bonny and apparently they both communicated well.

Rosa stated, *That she fills with warmth and happiness when she thinks of Dean. She can't bear him to be sad and is glad he has me to help him through. She wasn't jealous of our relationship because she knew one day she wouldn't be there for him and needed to know there was someone she could trust to look after him. She said we did the right thing putting her to*

*sleep and she is grateful. She didn't know how old
she was, but said she lived a full and happy life as
long as it should have been. She was always
amused by Bonny the cat and thought her a bit of a
clown. However Bonny came across to the
communicator as very sensible. She said she
missed Rosa, but life goes on and so she is not
going to waste it by grieving. She remembers the
good times and wants to make more good times in
the future.*

It brought some comfort as she continued
to accurately describe Rosa's personality. However
losing our beloved Rosa was just the first Wave of
loss.

***

In January 2011, I was in work at my desk when
my brother Robert rang me. It was very unusual to
hear from him, especially at work, but I presumed
he was ringing to wish me happy birthday. I knew
he was recovering well but there was still concern
for him. However he came straight out and told
me that Alex was ill, he had lung cancer and it was
serious. Alex had asked if Robert could ring as it
was too difficult to tell his sisters. I couldn't stay
on the phone as I had to gather myself and I
literally couldn't think straight. I sat at my desk
and wondered what to do.

I worked in an office environment that had
no soul. The people around me preferred to listen
to the sound of their own voices, so couldn't hear
my quietly desperate call for help. This was a

serious situation, no mountain out of a mole hill here, but as I would discover, office drama kings and queens don't like being upstaged by real shit.

Large open plan offices suggest freedom and engagement, but in fact they can foster a lack of care and support amongst staff, as there is no privacy and it is easy for people not to get involved, as they can hide behind their screens and leave it for someone else to deal with.

I can only presume this is why no-one ever approached me and asked how I was throughout the following months when my brother's illness weighed very heavy on me. It was dismal, my appetite reduced to that of a mouse, and I needed a glass of wine before I could eat anything. Alex was going to have treatment so this gave us all some hope.

I was crossing the road outside my work a few days later and thinking about everything that was going on. I started running to make sure I made it across in time, and heard a voice in my head shout "Stop!" It was a command and spoken with absolute authority but quietly. I stopped immediately and a car came racing past. I had misjudged the direction of the traffic and would have run straight into it. That voice saved my life. I have read that we have junctions throughout our lives where we can opt out early if life becomes too difficult, often through accident or illness. I was a step away from departing in that moment, and in a way it encouraged me to try hard to hold myself together. I wasn't ready to go.

Alex continued with treatment and we

hoped for a good outcome, especially as the treatment was quite new.

It's now May 2011 and I'm back at my desk at work. Maggie's younger sister, Heather, sent me a message through Facebook asking me to ring her, saying it wasn't good news. I rang her immediately.

My friend Maggie had been found dead in her own house a few days ago and she had been trying to find out how to get in touch with me. I couldn't believe it; there I was, sitting at the same desk where only in January I had been told about Alex's cancer which I had talked to Maggie about. I was in a state of utter disbelief. I spoke to a male colleague next to me, telling him a close friend had just died and he just looked at me blankly. What was wrong with these people? I decided to leave and go home. I couldn't stay there a moment longer. I felt physically sick and avoided everyone I passed. Maggie was supposed to be coming to the Scottish Isle of Bute in June with Dean's band who were playing at a festival. We'd planned it for ages.

We last stayed with Maggie in Scotland the previous July, on our return from a visit to Arran, an island Maggie had spoken fondly of for years. Maggie was a superb cook, and used the best ingredients she could afford to make delicious meals, patiently, cooked to perfection. Her Tarragon Chicken dish was famous. We joked that it clinched it when I made it for Dean when we met, and Heather also cooked it for her new man in the early days. They are married now with two children. We enjoyed excellent food and great music, and settled around a bonfire with a drink and a smoke. Maggie's compilations were legendary. She was an alchemist, and chose the perfect selection of tracks to conjure memories of hazy, summer days, enjoying a spliff and some beers with friends in the open countryside. She knew the ingredients for a great time together and was definitely one of my hedonistic friends.

I stayed in close contact with Heather whilst she tried to find out what had happened from professionals in the field of sudden death, whilst making arrangements for Maggie's funeral. Heather is one of those superwomen who seem to effortlessly manage anything that is thrown at them in life, whilst being an attentive mother, daughter, sister, wife and business woman. She is bonny and petite but made of pure dynamite.

It seemed that a concoction of prescription drugs for sleep, muscle pain and alcohol had created a toxic brew which put poor Maggie into a sleep that she couldn't wake up from. She was only 42. I travelled alone, taking the train up to her funeral in Ayrshire, Then I was gratefully ensconced in the bosom of her family after Heather picked me up from the station, dropping me back a few days later. It helped me get through the service and return home, knowing I would always have a connection to her through her family.

Margaret, as she was called by her family, would be hugely missed. She had her demons to fight, as we all do, but she had a courageous and generous heart. Her love of Scotland was infectious; she would talk about special places intimately and make me want to visit them.

The trip to Bute went ahead as planned; the band were playing at a festival. On the ferry crossing over from Wemyss Bay to Bute I went on deck with a few others and we sprinkled roses on the sea for Maggie. At exactly that moment, a seagull appeared above us and hovered magically for a few minutes then flew off when we were done. Dean dedicated a song to Maggie called "Turn out the Light", saying he hoped she was here with us somewhere; it was very emotional. That was the second Wave of loss.

***

In July we went to Italy for a week, a trip that had been planned for a long time. As we arrived in Venice and waited for a bus to take us to our hotel, I got a call from Judith to tell me that Alex's health had deteriorated, and the cancer had aggressively advanced. In hindsight I wish I hadn't brought my phone with me, as we needed respite from the worry and heartache.

My sister kindly rang me to ask if I was okay as she'd had the same news and knew I was away from home. A dark cloud cast itself over any attempt to displace my brother's illness, so that was that. However, of all the places in the world, Venice was probably a good place to unravel. It was the 'Art Biennale' (contemporary visual arts exhibition), so the beautiful, old buildings throughout Venice were used to house spectacular, thought-provoking and sometimes humorous installations. We spent each day crossing decorative stone bridges that rose above the watery highways, amidst stunning scenery, and beautiful statues. It reached into my heart, despite my sorrow. The bejewelled and candle-lit interiors of the ancient churches offered solace and understanding. Traversing the bridges felt like a metaphor for the final crossing Alex would be making soon, though nobody knew when. It hung like a heavy, sword above me; I'd find myself irrepressibly crying, in a restaurant, lying on the beach or contemplating a piece of art. Such is the Italian disposition, the Venetians just took it in their stride, and the tourists were too busy trying to find their way around to even notice.

We were staying outside of Venice itself, on the Lido, at a family run hotel that served ambient music along with a plentiful breakfast. I'm sure the music helped me find my appetite as I was struggling to eat. A peaceful calm pervaded the place; the staff appeared to glide around us, topping up milk and juices, and replenishing trays of food.

A few days into our holiday, I was waiting downstairs for Dean before heading out into Venice in the late afternoon. There was a miniscule bar in the lobby, so I sat on the only seat and ordered a glass of wine. Despite the heat, I wore an overcoat of dread as I thought of Alex's plight and wondered how I would cope with losing him. It was too soon and so unexpected. I asked for a sign from my mother to help me. As I stared over the top of the bar, I noticed a poem the size of a postcard, framed and hung on the wall. It read;

La farfalla non contra I mesi ma gli attimi e il tempo le basta

The butterfly counts not months but moments and has time enough

R Tagore

It touched me deeply, and it felt like a 'reply' to my thoughts; I decided I'd put it in the card to Alex that I would send from Venice.

Dean then appeared, spruced up and ready to go. We walked outside and were met by a huge rainbow arching above us, yet there was no sunshine or rain to create it. I thought again of my mother and felt it was a reassuring sign from her to say I wasn't on my own however much it felt like it.

Later that day, I took myself off to compose my letter to Alex whilst Dean climbed to the top of St Mark's Campanile, the bell tower of St Mark's Basilica. I sat on a stone seat outside the Cathedral away from the tourists that constantly clogged the arteries of Venice. Hidden away under the cool, stone arches, I could still my mind and write from my heart. After posting my card there was nothing more to do than surrender to the beauty and charm of the place.

When we left Venice we caught the train to Pisa before flying back from there to Newcastle. We were very low on money and were trying not to use our credit card to avoid charges. There were a few hours to kill before our flight and we were hungry, so we headed into Pisa to see if we could find a cheap snack. On the way, I spotted a 10 Euro note on the ground which, when added to our change, meant we could share a pasta in a nearby café/restaurant. Mysteriously, the only one we could afford was the "Farfalla" dish which was made with pasta shaped like butterflies, and it made me think of the poem I'd read.

***

Alex fought the lung cancer stoically and maintained his humour and sharp wit. We visited him in Scotland after being told he had cancer. When I first saw him I remember walking towards his front door ready to hug him; I could "see" the cancer in him like a yellow, rubbery alien, and I knew it had a strong hold. I just wanted to run away and keep running, not wanting any of it to be true, I felt like such a coward. Alex was still very handsome despite having lost weight. His skin had a different hue, and it became apparent he grew easily tired, and would take himself off to his room to lie down, but it was so good to be with him.

Alex went into the Royal Navy aged 16 years old; he lived in Gibraltar, visited the Falklands and travelled around Europe. When he left, 9 years later, he picked up the loose threads of his education and quickly wove himself a path towards University where he studied a degree in Psychology at Newcastle then moved to Manchester for a job in academia. He set up life there for a few years and met a German woman who he was going to live with, but she broke his heart. Alex wasn't the type to leave himself wide open to being wounded in love, but there is no accounting for betrayal. She betrayed him badly.

Alex was a sweet man and had a higher than average understanding of the nuances and foibles of women, no doubt due to his close relationship with his sisters. He would see his ex with her new partner, as they all worked in the same place of work, but he eventually gave himself a break and took a job and a fresh start in Dundee. Alex wandered, wounded, in an emotional desert for a few years, concentrating on his work which he loved, but from what I can gather, salvation came in the form of a band called [11]Dreadzone and its loyal and hearty followers. Alex had always loved his music and was a great and unabashed dancer. The band's music was an uplifting formula of reggae/dub/trance/ambient and the band and their followers were all about bringing everyone together and feeling connected, travelling the UK to gather at gigs and spend the night dancing, then socialising afterwards with the band and catching up with each other.

Thankfully it wasn't long before he found love again with a woman called Judith. She had a daughter already and before the life-changing news on Alex's health they had another daughter who was now 2 years old.

Alex and Judith had planned to get married, but it was impossible for them to arrange. I asked

Alex directly if I could arrange their marriage, and after a short chat with Judith he said, "Yes if that was alright." Which it was. I felt so helpless but was grateful to have something I could do.

Scottish law is different, and on this occasion it worked in our favour; there seemed less red tape than I was expecting. I rang the local Registrar's office and started the ball rolling, packing my conversation with a heartfelt desire to achieve this as soon as possible due to the difficult circumstances. It was hard listening to myself explain to a stranger on the phone the reasons behind the urgency of the wedding; it made the finality more real and just sounded so sad.

Ruth drove up from Dorset to stay with Alex and Judith to sort out all the paperwork and liaise with the Registrar's office. Between us we arranged the wedding in a week.

The wedding ceremony was intense and intimate. The rain lashed down all day long, reflecting the reservoir of grief damming up inside us all. A young nephew gave Judith away to Alex, while Robert and his son gave beautiful and courageous readings. Dean kindly recorded the ceremony from the back on a video camera. Alex looked emotional but held it together, entertaining us with a wee flick of his kilt. The marriage would bring Alex some peace of mind, knowing that his family would be financially secure and have a beautiful home to live in thanks to his hard work and commitment over the years.

Just over 9 weeks later on 28 September 2011, Alex drifted quickly and quietly into the next world from his bed with his new wife sleeping beside him. I was in London for work and staying in a Premier Inn. I remember briefly waking around 6 am and thinking of him. I don't know what time he died, but it was sometime in the early hours. I had an early phone call with Robert when he told me the heart-breaking news. I hated being in London. Scotland felt a long way away; if I was back in Newcastle I would feel closer to him. A sword had been dangling over my head for months, and had finally dropped. I had fretted over when I would get *The Call,* where I would be and who I would be with. It seemed important while I was waiting for the sword to drop, but none of it mattered in the end. Fortunately for me Carla was close at hand as she was living in London, so I arranged to stay with her. She left work early to meet me and take me back to hers. I didn't want to be on my own; I couldn't think straight about anything, so she was a Godsend. We would travel back to Newcastle together the next day.

***

I don't think I could have watched my brother being buried if Dean hadn't been one of the people carrying him, as they always got on very well and somehow having Dean in the frame made it possible to bear. My Dad also carried his son, which must have been hard. He made a trip up to see Alex when he heard he was very ill. They hadn't had any contact for many years, so I was proud of him on both accounts.

Friends who attended told me they thought it was a beautiful funeral, but for me personally it was one of the most difficult things I have done in my adult life to date. Judith had asked if I wanted to read something but I was too grief stricken to consider it; instead I chose the music after checking with Robert and Ruth over my choices. Music was a really big thing for me and Alex so it felt appropriate. I didn't get to talk to Alex much when he was ill, and yet in the past we had talked about everything so it was odd to have not discussed such an important matter, and I felt very guilty that we hadn't. In retrospect I think if he had wanted to he would have. I sent him beautiful cards instead to tell him how I felt about him and to offer my support, however futile it felt at the time.

Just before he was buried and after much agonizing, I decided to visit Alex in his bedroom where he lay in a wicker coffin. I was kindly accompanied by my cousin Mark who had sadly said goodbye to both his parents by now. My sister had seen Alex and I was worried I might regret it. He still looked very handsome, but I subsequently suffered post-traumatic shock. I struggled with him being being buried and not cremated. However, three things really helped me in those first few weeks that followed; swimming, [12]Death Cafe and a lady called Barbara.

***

I was swimming 2-3 times a week. Under the water became the only place I felt safe and comfortable. I was away from everything and everyone, and I felt closest to Alex and my Mam. It was solace for my mind, body and soul. I could chat away to them in my head whilst flying through the blue water which felt like sky. It felt like a gigantic womb where I could access the spiritual world . Lucy and I went swimming a lot at that time. We would catch up briefly in the pool. It was a good place to discuss difficult feelings, because I could duck under the water if I got really upset. Lucy was gentle company and would suggest I join her and her partner Thomas and have tea at her house when Dean was away. It was a lifesaver.

Death Cafe is a real, pop-up cafe with tea, coffee and cakes and also offers support online. Professionals who deal with death and dying eg Embalmers, Crematorium staff, Palliative care nurses, Priests, etc are invited along to give talks and answer the sort of questions you can't ask a family member. I asked some very difficult questions around Alex's final care and received sensitive and well informed replies that helped me put some fears to rest. It is a great opportunity to seek answers to questions that keep you awake at night.

Barbara Meiklejohn-Free is a medium, and she was participating in a psychic fayre held in Newcastle. She was giving a Mediumship demonstration and I decided to go.

There were lots of people seated and

waiting expectantly, hoping to receive a message. By now I'd seen a number of mediums, so I wasn't phased by the idea. Barbara was giving some good, strong and clear messages that were received with humour and understanding. I didn't expect to receive one as it was literally 18 days since we had buried Alex. I was starting to get annoyed because one young woman at the front was now receiving her third lengthy message. It was coming to a close and Barbara was only giving one more message. Suddenly she began pacing up and down and saying this is really important, I need to find this person, I have to pass this message on. It went something like this:-

"I have been shown a flower, it's a rose. Can anyone relate to that?" A few people put their hands up, including me, given it was my name.

Barbara continued. "Who has visited a grave recently?"
I kept my hand up, as did the lady right next to me. It was Barbara's job to establish who the message was for, though I knew without any doubt it was for me so felt a bit sorry for the lady next to me.

She explained she had a woman and a man and the woman was saying "He isn't in the ground, he is here! They are together now and although chalk and cheese (which is true) they fit together really well. I didn't know the woman so well, but I knew the man well", she stated. "He passed over very recently and is finding it all new and wondering what he is doing here and how it all works".

Well this was Alex all over; he was very

bright and would patiently take his time to work things out. He enjoyed undoing knotted silver chains and had sorted mine out a few times. However, I needed more evidence; this was not a time to be taken advantage of. I was too raw and vulnerable.

"I'm being given the letter A, and the name Alex, not Alec but Alex, he is very clear about that", continued Barbara.

I couldn't believe what I was hearing and yes Alex was particular about people saying his name right, he wasn't an Alec or an Alexander. Now we were cooking on gas.

She stated I'd experienced three losses not just one, to which I nodded, remembering our beloved Rosa and Maggie. Barbara revealed that he had joked with me years ago when we were talking about death that he would come back and tell me if it was true that life continued, because he didn't believe it did. He told Barbara to tell me "It is real!".

Barbara further relayed important evidence that Alex was there and would always be around me or never far away. One of the things that was really upsetting me was that I didn't get to give Alex a proper, big hug when I last saw him in his bedroom with Robert and Ruth. I had sat next to him on his bed and put my arm around him and told him we all love him but that was all. It was desperately hard leaving his room, knowing inside I wasn't going to see him again.

The hall was deafeningly silent as Barbara explained she was struggling to speak from the emotion between Alex and myself. Then she set off walking round the edge of the room which was a considerable size. She walked towards the back then behind the row of chairs where I was seated and said, "I just need to do this for some reason", and asked me to stand up, and she gave me the most wonderful hug saying, "He needed to give you a hug".

It was an amazing lift to my diminished spirit and I thanked Barbara from my heart. I was so grateful to Alex and so proud of his ability to communicate to me and so soon after his death.

When I stepped outside into daylight to wait for a lift home, everything looked different, the trees and sky were shimmering as if they weren't really solid. Barbara had opened up a portal for me that day and given me a glimpse into another world that had been an incredible experience.

So that was the third and final Wave, making up what I can only describe as a tidal wave of loss. I cried for a whole year on and off, so much so that I gave up wearing mascara. So many times I would try and get ready to go out to socialise and I would end up sobbing and having to start again. It was a tough climb, especially at work. I was exhausted and had lost about two stone from not eating, but no-one in the huge open-plan office seemed to notice. I made a promise to myself there and then that I would not be working in the same job by the time I was 50. Alex had died aged 50 and Maggie aged 42, and life was too precious to be doing a job where I wasn't valued, understood, respected or fulfilled. I had 5 years to sort it out.

Later that year during the latest of many office restructures, I left my desk to occupy one in a different part of the office. I wanted to smash my desk up for the devastating and heart breaking news I had received whilst sitting at it, and the total lack of care and support I'd received from the so-called colleagues around me. Funnily enough a guy from Building Works came in and did just that. The new desks were required to be smaller, so the old, big ones had to be broken up and thrown away. I asked him if I could smash it up, but being a total 'Jobs worth' he wouldn't let me.

Dancing with Alex

At the top of my street was a Spiritual Church. I'd been to them many years ago, so I knew the format. I was a bit apprehensive because I still felt so raw, but I couldn't resist the possibility of contact with Alex or Maggie.

It was an Open Circle night, which meant experienced and budding mediums would pass messages to members of the audience and each other.

I remembered seeing a guy called Jeff about 25 years ago at another church, and who I thought had been very good, not only in his accuracy, but the kindly manner he imparted his information.

I walked into the building, sat myself down and couldn't believe it. Jeff was there. After the usual prayers, the circle was opened for receiving messages. Jeff passed on messages, he was as good as I remembered, and I was sure he would have something for me, but it wasn't to be. Other mediums of all ages and experience delivered their messages to the anticipating congregation. Soon it was over and time for tea and biscuits. I went to get up to leave, as I didn't feel like talking to anyone, when Jeff came to the end of my row and asked if he could speak to me.

"Of course, please join me", and I gestured for him to shuffle along to the free seat next to me.

"I didn't want to give you this information publicly as I felt it would be too much for you," he sensitively explained. Then he continued to share his message;

"You know someone who passed with complications, found something here (pointing to his chest), then somewhere else, then found out it was worse, you knew it was inevitable. He had cancer." I nodded slowly.

"He knew he wasn't well but just ignored it." I nodded again, as this was something I had recently been thinking.

"The sun will come again", offered Jeff, "There has been a lot of rain, in the form of tears, but a plant needs sunshine to grow and it will shine again." "He loved looking out of the window at the sunshine. You have a photo standing up of him, he's blowing you a kiss now as you have blown a kiss to his photograph". Both statements were entirely true, and as is often the case with this communication, there was a deeper meaning in the message, like a hidden gem, because one of the songs I had chosen for Alex's funeral was [13]Here Comes the Sun' by the Beatles. I felt he was making a reference to that, as well as telling me I will be happy again after all the crying. Alex had a wonderful view of rural Scotland from his bedroom window where he spent all of his time, towards the end.

Jeff continued, "He is alright now, as he has been in a hospital for the mind to get rid of the effects of illness". This last bit of information intrigued me as well as giving me comfort. I thanked him for his time and told him that I had thought of him and hoped to see him, but really hadn't expected to. He was taken aback by this as he hadn't visited this particular church for ages.

Messages certainly help, but nothing can take away the fact you have to carry on with your life after losing someone you've loved. In the early days you just have to eat, sleep and do what you need to do to function. There's no magic formula, though it is important to talk to other human beings, whether strangers or friends. There comes a desire not to think about the loss *all* the time, and eventually you notice that for a small part of the day you haven't been fixated on feelings of grief. Those small moments get longer, and eventually less of each day is given over to dwelling on your loss, but that can take months or even years. Strangely I found that when I was brushing my teeth it was impossible not to think about it. Is it because I'm looking in the mirror seeing my troubled reflection, or perhaps the nature of the task is beyond distraction?

In December of 2011 the Dreadzone crew that Alex was part of arranged to gather together at a gig in Bristol to honour Alex their "brother". I debated going but Dean wasn't free and I just couldn't muster the confidence to go alone, having never met anyone there. I heard later the band had spoken a heartfelt tribute to Alex and dedicated a song to him, which was lovely to know, and I berated myself for not going. I did go and see them in March 2012 in Leeds with Dean at my side, then met the band afterwards. It was only after meeting them I found out the guy who led the band had lost his own brother who had been a band member, so there was a real empathy with him.

Later that year I travelled alone to Bristol to see them play. I wanted to see Alex's friends who had gathered in his memory the previous December, as I still regretted not having gone.

Anxiety was still curling my edges, so I was really nervous about a solo flight to Bristol and my emotions were already running high at the prospect of meeting his friends, as I didn't want to be overcome with sadness and embarrass myself.

The flight was the worst I've experienced. Bristol airport is notoriously windy, and it took three attempts to land as we were flying in a thunderstorm in the dark. There was an uncanny silence on the plane as people turned within to calm their fears. I was sure I could visualise myself at the gig that night, so I remained optimistic that we would land safely at Bristol and not have to divert elsewhere, and eventually we did.

I caught the airport bus into Bristol and was listening to a man on his mobile who had a strong Geordie accent. He came off his phone and turned round and was staring at me. Then he got up and came over and spoke enquiringly. "Rose?" I looked into his face and slowly realized it was Harry from my Hotel Management class at Newcastle College.

"Yes it is, hello Harry", and gave him a hug. Then the next thing he said totally threw me.

"How's your brother?"

I explained that he had died and I was coming to see his much loved band and hopefully meet some of his friends. He knew the band, and said they were great as he'd seen them before and we reminisced about time spent at Alex's flat. It felt like a sign from Alex telling me he was around.

Harry said he lived in India and flies to Russia and other countries quite regularly with his work, and that he nearly put himself in the brace position on the flight we'd shared from Newcastle. This made me laugh so much. I had been none the wiser how bad it actually was.

We exchanged numbers and went our separate ways. I headed to my cousin Martin's house, where I was staying, and got myself turned around ready for the gig which Martin was accompanying me to. Before the band went on I literally bumped into Greg the drummer. It was going to be a special night.

The gig was fantastic, the room was packed with people and good vibes. I danced the whole time. Whilst dancing to the song Alex's wife had chosen to play at his funeral, I noticed someone to my far left who on first glance was the absolute spit of Alex; he even danced in the same way. It was extraordinary. I felt I was dancing with my brother having never been to a Dreadzone gig with Alex before, and it was wonderful. I met with his friends after the gig and we all went to say hello to the band. Greg told me he had put "[14]Changes" in the set for me, the song they'd played as a tribute for Alex. It was so thoughtful and helped me stop beating myself up for not attending it.

"Be bold and mighty forces will come to your aid…." It might not seem much, but making that journey to the gig, at that time was a really big deal for me given the anxiety I was suffering, and I had been well- rewarded emotionally and spiritually.

Heavenly Reunion

As her daughter Rose had predicted in a card to her brother, Margaret was right there with Alex when he died. She was accompanied by many others, but it was her face she wanted him to see when he crossed over to help him understand what had happened. It was a case of here today, gone tomorrow; his energy had powered down over the months so his transition into spirit was seamless.

He awoke to his mother's serene gaze, as she sat patiently at his bedside. The effects of the cancer meant he would need to rest in a hospital to clear the emotional 'scars' and avoid feeling increasingly depleted and prone to despondency, following his separation from the people he loved on Earth. Alex was overjoyed to see his mother again and smiled back at her with the whole of his being. His scientific outlook hadn't prepared him for this, so it was it was a lot to take onboard.

Margaret's presence flitted in and out of Alex's consciousness between long periods of deep rest. He went for short walks with her in serene gardens by a river. Friends and family who had died came to visit him, including the family dog, Red. The handsome Red Setter looked in perfect health and would appear anytime Alex thought of him. Alex found he was able to communicate telepathically with everyone, including Red, who thanked Alex for looking after him and ensuring he was given to a family that had really cared for him. Red's coat shimmered, and when Alex stroked him flashes of light flicked off in every direction, displaying his joy at their reunion.

It wasn't too long before Alex himself was recovered and in glowing health. He missed his family and friends greatly, but having his mother by his side lessened the grief. She inducted him to heaven and taught him about the workings of the Universe alongside his own guide Kanna, just as Orker had shown her when she first arrived back. With her experience and guidance he was quick to learn the basics and settled back easily. He wanted to visit Earth as soon as possible, as he felt there were some things left unfinished with members of his family.

St Georges Church in Jesmond, Newcastle, was where his parents and other members of his family had got married. He and his siblings had been christened there and every year a Church fete was held on the Church green. His mother wasn't religious but ensured we all joined in with community activities, which also allowed her to catch up with old friends who she'd see there. The whole family would go, as there were stalls and entertainment for every age from shooting a football through a hole to the White Elephant stall. Alex knew his brother and sisters held great memories of this event, so it was here where he chose to 'bring' Ruth, Rose and Robert to meet up with him, aided by their guides, through the gateway of their dreams.

All four of them lay down on the luscious grass of St George's Church Green with their heads near each other, forming a four-pointed star and gazing upwards into a sublime blue sky. It was a summer's day back in 1974. No words were exchanged, but the joy of sharing the memories washed over their souls and would help them cope with their earthly separation from Alex. Margaret stayed back from this event as the Earth's atmosphere had a denseness that Alex was still acclimatised to, but Margaret would have needed Orker's support to stay, and he was unavailable.

This connection would help Alex heal enormously. Ruth was particularly receptive to Alex's presence in her dream state, and would likely remember the meeting when she awoke, which would bring her great comfort.

He had already lined up a visit to Rose because he knew she would shortly be seeing an excellent medium, and he hoped to get a message through if he could master how to. Rose was interested in life after death; it was a subject they had discussed on a number of occasions.

Alex visited his young daughter Lake every night in her dreams. She was only 2 years old, so her mind was wide open and she didn't question his appearances; instead she looked forward to playing hide and seek and speaking to him with her toys. He also made contact with his wife and his older daughter at this time, but it wasn't so easy as there was a lot of grief to penetrate.

Following his own life review, Alex chose to combine his excellent research skills with his personal experience, as a victim of cancer, to develop improvements for cancer patients on Earth. He was still more comfortable in a university environment and would be working in a team who were dedicated to exploring revolutionary treatments to eradicate cancer. Their ideas would be communicated to receptive health professionals and other interested individuals on Earth, through inspiration and guidance. Alex's contribution as a recent sufferer would be invaluable.

Universities were different in Heaven. For a start, he had access to the greatest minds there have ever been. Lectures could be given by Marie Curie or Albert Einstein, and students were encouraged to spend time with these enlightened souls in their chosen field of study, so the opportunity to learn was unparalleled. It suited Alex to continue learning and researching because he had died carrying an unfulfilled desire to achieve more in this field.

**

"Hullo there, how are you?" Alex turned round to see Maggie standing in his doorway.

"Well hello Maggie, its good to see you, this is all a bit strange" he confessed.

"Just take your time with it all, dinnae worry, you'll be fine. Would you like to come out to a concert?"

"Yeah why not?" He was struck by how well Maggie looked. She had always been an attractive woman but now she really glowed with health. Her pale skin and golden brown hair had a lustre to it that was otherworldly.

Alex had known Maggie, Rose's friend; they'd had a brief relationship and remained friends afterwards. They shared a passion for music, so it wasn't going to be too long before she showed up to welcome him and invite him out to a musical event he wouldn't forget.

"The concerts here are amazing, Alex. It helped me when I first arrived back. I know you'll be missing everyone, so let's go and have a wee bit of fun."

"What should I wear?" Alex enquired, having given no thought to his attire since arriving as there had been more pressing matters to focus on.

Maggie giggled. "Just imagine an outfit you'd like to wear and it will appear; you can change your mind anyway".

He thought of an outfit he used to like when he was younger and fitter, jeans, white, cap-sleeved T-shirt and his black Harrington jacket with Doctor Martens on his feet.

"Okay I'm ready!" he announced. "What do we do now?"

Maggie threw him a mischievous smile whilst replying, "Just follow me and I'll get us there. Better not keep Bob Marley waiting".

American Freedom and Wonder Tour

When I last visited Alex, I spoke to him about a trip to America that I was planning; he had been there many times through his work. I used to quiz him about it as I had a fascination with the place and the people, possibly due to the American series '[16]Starsky and Hutch', which I was fanatical about as a child. When he first visited I asked him to bring me back something "really American", and he brought me a '[17]Twinkie' and a baseball.

He wisely suggested I consider which America I wanted to experience as there were so many aspects to the country. I knew it was the land itself I wanted to see, not the theme parks or the shopping malls. My plan was embryonic, but it was an easier subject to talk about than cancer, and he appeared to welcome the distraction.

After Alex died some of his belongings became keepsakes that were shared within our family. I came across a photo of Alex sitting outside 'The Cloud Gate' in Chicago, a giant silver sculpture by Indian- born British artist Sir Anish Kapoor, referred to locally as the 'Bean' or 'Silver Bean'. He looked really happy and I knew I wanted to start my journey right there.

On 2nd April 2012, Dean and I flew to Chicago to begin our "Freedom and Wonder Tour". The aim of the trip was to remind myself that the world is a wonderful place. We visited the "Silver Bean" on a glorious sunny day, so we saw it at its best. After two nights in Chicago, we headed west on the train from Union Station, riding on the 'California Zephyr', one of Amtrak's most appealing train journeys. Crossing over the plains of Nebraska and Denver, then climbing up to the Rockies I looked down on the nest of a Bald Eagle, and through the snow-capped Sierra Nevadas. Powering on to San Francisco for the final stop. As we progressed towards our destination we smashed through time zones. I was suspended in time, giving me much needed distance from my life back home.

The Manager of the 'Zephyr' ran a tight ship. Gwendolyn was the go-to lady for our carriage, she was a super woman. She was a tall black lady with an easy manner and a perceptive eye. She kept us under her wing for the whole 2400 miles. She worked hard and yet kept her sassy sense of humour throughout. She sensed immediately we were new to the Amtrak experience.

The dining car was meticulously run. Meals were served skillfully and promptly. The waiting staff shuffled the customers up like a pack of cards and dealt us a different dining experience at every sitting We met people from all over who chose to take the train for many different reasons. Some didn't like to fly, some just loved the train, others said it was the cheapest way to visit their relatives. We had breakfast with a couple from West Kilbride, Ayrshire, very close to where my friend Maggie had lived, which made me think of her. Then we met a couple heading home to Sacramento called Jim and Ann who we really hit it off with. Their company was like the Key Lime

Pie, light, satisfying and really enjoyable. We spent our remaining meals with them and met up in the evening at the viewing car for Jim Beam and ginger, and to pore over maps so they could give us some useful steers for our route ahead. As we disembarked for the last time I pushed some dollars and a pack of biscuits into Gwendolyn's hands, because she told us she was dizzy from working so long without food, and we thanked her for looking after us so well.

"Just giving you both a little jumpstart", she responded. Then we headed for the bus into San Francisco.

It was a place of contrasts. The past and future lived side by side. Golden rays of "flower power" shone out from Haight & Ashbury onto the global visitors as they crammed onto the old trams to tourist hot spots, the Fisherman's Wharf and Union Square. There were echoes of Beatnik prose in the bars and bookshops of North Beach district. Saint Francis himself might be pleased with how San Francisco embraced diverse and minority lifestyles, though sadly this did not reach to the many homeless and drug-addled casualties tucked away in the shadows or reduced to begging on street corners to survive. Across the river, Sausolito, with its laid back vibe, offered welcome peace from the buzz of the City Lights.

On the fifth day, Dean and I picked up a hire car and started south towards our next destination, Yosemite National Park. The travelling around and daily planning focused me on new subjects and helped me to think differently, but the loss of Alex, 6 months on, was sitting dormant, underneath my thoughts, ready to emerge without warning. I hoped for some small sign to connect me to him.

We took the advice of our 'Zephyr' companions Ann and Jim who said we should visit Monterey, where we could book a boat trip to see the migrating grey whales. As we made our way in that direction we spotted a couple of young dudes thumbing for a ride. We scooped them up and welcomed them aboard.

"Hi guys, where are you heading?" Dean enquired.
"Just into Santa Cruz man, thanks for the lift, we're pretty tired", the older lad replied.

"I'm Dean and this is my partner Rose" Dean offered up.

"My name's Alex and this is Wan". Dean and I shot glances at each other.

"Where are you going yourselves?" Alex asked. Dean described our plans to '[18]Bill and Ted', and I pondered the coincidence of one of them being my brother's namesake as they chattered on in the background.

***

One of the wonderful aspects of being dead was that Alex could travel to anywhere in the world in the blink of an eye.

He had mastered the ability to 'join' family members at will and had been practising different ways to communicate with them and to pass on important information.

His younger sister Rose was on a big trip to America. She had talked to him about it when he was alive and he was keen to let her know he was with her.

San Francisco is a portal between heaven and earth, so it is particularly easy for souls to 'cross over', though it can be very congested with many comings and goings.

He transports himself down and joins Rose and her partner Dean in the back of their hire car as they drive down the West Coast of America. He seeks the assistance of a couple of stoners who are meandering along trying to decide what to do with their day. The marijuana they've just smoked has opened their minds, making it easy for Alex to drop in the suggestion to hitch a lift to Santa Cruz, where they are from, and head to their local bar for a game of pool and a few beers. One of them is called Alex and he's certain this would mean something to Rose. He just has to time his communication so that Rose and Dean will pick them up as they pass by, because he knows they wouldn't drive by without offering them a lift, and he was right.

***

My reverie was broken as our two young hitchers got ready to disembark. The older looking one, called Alex, handed me a wild, yellow flower as he thanked us and climbed out; it felt like a gift from my brother. A surge of grief rose up inside me but

I kept the lid firmly on and thanked him very much. I placed the flower on the dashboard and we continued towards Monterey to see the whales.

Unfortunately when we got there it was raining hard and no more boats were going out that day. We covered up and took a short walk along the coast instead.

I spotted a couple of sea otters basking side by side on their backs in the water, holding on to each other with one paw so they wouldn't drift apart in their sleep. It was delightful to watch, and reminded me that sometimes in the middle of the night, when my fears arose, I put a hand on Dean to tether myself to him and prevent me 'floating' off into darkness, a small action that grounded me through the night.

We were in John Steinbeck country, so we decided to take refuge from the downpour and visit the Steinbeck Museum in Salinas. It was a real treasure trove of American life. We spent hours there, and when we emerged my earlier grief, along with the deluge, had subsided. We had crossed the Diablo Range.

If you take a wrong turn in America it can lead you miles out of your way, and we took several. It was early evening, and we eventually arrived at the Comfort Inn, Oakhurst, which thankfully I'd booked ahead. There was a bar next door called the Dirty Donkey where we had a few 'big ones' with a couple of locals, then got an early night. The next day we were visiting Yosemite National Park.

It was early morning on 11th April 2012

and the weather looked clear and bright. We filled up with bagels, waffles and coffee and set off for Yosemite. As the car climbed higher, the temperature grew colder. By the time we reached the entrance, the ground was white from a light snowfall. We made our way up the winding path to Mariposa Grove to see the giant sequoias.

These trees were colossal and soared up towards the heavens. One of them had an arch at the base which we could walk through together. It was amazing to think that Jesus Christ could have walked past these ancient trees had he lived in this part of the world. They were the Elders of the land. The snow was falling more generously now as we headed back down the road to the car park. We drove towards the centre of the park, and entered a long tunnel that eventually propelled us into the stunning view of an endless valley with large cliffs either side. We accompanied the river to its cascading waterfall, passing a lonesome coyote standing at the side of the road, bravely standing his ground when we parked up close to watch him.

We spent the whole day exploring the park and regretted not booking an overnight stay as the accommodation was full. As dusk fell we reluctantly drove back through the tunnel to exit. When we emerged the weather was severe. The roads were completely white and we were in a blizzard. Dean slowed right down but kept going as we passed cars marooned at the roadside as drivers waited it out. Every vehicle had chains on their tyres, which we had arrogantly ignored, along with the fifty dollar charge. Our hire car was not safe and likely to slip off the road and down the banks. There were no guard rails what-so-ever, this was America, not prudent Britain.

I became really scared; we hadn't prepared for a white out. I prayed for help. The temperature was freezing and there were bears around; sleeping in the car was not an option. I tried to ring a ranger but my phone wouldn't connect. Dean was in a quandary, but eventually agreed to turn round to attempt to get back to the tunnel.

Alex was aware that Rose and Dean were in danger, and he was close by to come to their aid. He had already whispered in their ears to turn back and fortunately they had heard. He just needed to persuade the only ranger in the area to drive out towards them and guide them to safety.

Visibility was atrocious, but we reached the tunnel and re-emerged to much clearer weather. The tunnel was like something out of The Lion, the Witch and the Wardrobe, a doorway to another world. We knew the only hotel was fully booked, and didn't know how to safely get out of the park another way. I spotted a ranger in the distance attending to a sign, so we headed straight to him. Thankfully, he directed us towards an alternative exit we weren't aware of, which he said would take much longer but should be clear. It was a great relief, and I thanked him for answering my prayer. The road we took was much lower with little to no snow. It was a clear run back to our hotel as we gorged on beautiful vistas that we wouldn't have seen. It felt good to be alive. That evening we celebrated at the local Mexican diner with delicious food and copious margaritas.

The Tioga Pass is the highest mountain pass in the Sierra Nevada, and is in California. It was closed at this time of year because of snow, and after our experience in Yosemite we weren't going to attempt it. Instead our onward journey took us through Bakersfield, via Ridgecrest and on to Lone Pine, another place recommended by Jim and Ann, where we stayed for a few nights. This was cowboy country and our hotel proudly displayed a plaque saying John Wayne had stayed there.

From there we crossed Death Valley, doing a whirlwind tour of the sights; again we should have booked an overnight stay. Emotions were strained and the barren desert reflected our desolation perfectly. We continued to Las Vegas, arriving in multi-lane traffic at 9.30 pm at night. It had been an arduous journey and we hadn't booked anywhere. I defaulted to praying for help. Dean managed to park up at one of the giant hotels and I ran over to a kind looking porter to plead for directions to somewhere affordable. The guy was American and quickly deduced I was at the end of my tether.

"Okay lady, here we go", he instructed "This is what you need to do. Go out of here, take a right at the roundabout, follow the road down, look at for the big MGM hotel sign on your right but take the road opposite going off to the left. Up a short way and there's a Travel Lodge just on the right, and it won't clean you out, okay, you got it?"

I thanked him earnestly; he knew he'd played an important part and I was very grateful.

Las Vegas was everything we didn't like, noisy, false, overpriced, dirty and seedy. However, the gambler in me came to the fore and I jumped into a game of roulette and had the best time. The casinos, with their armies of machines and hostesses floating round delivering free drinks, made me wonder how many gamblers had lost their souls to so much temptation. It was sensation overload after the expansive landscape we'd just left.

On our second day before we departed, I insisted we visit the Bellagio fountains at the Bellagio Hotel and Casino. We waited patiently for the show to start, not knowing what to expect. Las Vegas had been fairly disappointing up to now. Even the guaranteed sunshine was nowhere to be seen; instead it had rained since we arrived, but the sun started to come out as the fountains began their display. Watching the water dance so euphorically, in perfect time to melodious symphonies, moved us both to tears, much to our surprise and it was a welcome release of the built-up stress from the last few days. I'm glad Las Vegas managed to reach inside us before we left. I'd like to return and stay in one of the themed hotels; it would appeal to my sense of fantasy. Now though it was time to leave.

We drove to the Hoover Dam and it was now a cloudless sunny day. The view from the top was astounding. It was easy to imagine why so many men had lost their lives during its construction. It was colossal. We crossed the bridge to put our toe in Arizona then back over to Nevada to head towards Utah. Our holiday feeling was restored; we were back in the flow, helped massively by the sudden change of scenery from manmade Las Vegas to desert plains and huge rock formations in the distance. They moved ever nearer until we were literally carving our way through them in the car.

Since Yosemite I hadn't pre-booked any accommodation so we were free to explore until we found somewhere we liked the look of, usually a motel at the side of the road. We found a place to stay in Springdale. Utah is a "dry state", but the guy on reception directed us to a Mexican restaurant within easy reach where we could get a beer. Zion National Park was nearby, and we arrived there early the next morning. A short train ride took you to the centre where we chose a trail through a Canyon; there were chipmunks everywhere. The highest trail was called "Angel's Landing". We met a local walker called "Kenny" who looked like he was made of bronze and very fit for his age. He told us that a man had recently fallen from Angel's Landing when he turned his back to the drop and lost his balance. His wife had tried to grab him but couldn't. That's when I decided we weren't doing it; I couldn't afford to lose anyone else, so it was vetoed, thanks to Kenny. He strongly suggested we do the Navajo Trail at Bryce Canyon though, which we were travelling to the following day.

I held a vain hope in the back of my mind that I might have an encounter with Native American Indian culture at some point, but as a white Western tourist it felt hidden away and protected from us, which was totally understandable. The Paiute Indians used to inhabit Bryce Canyon many thousands of years ago, but more recently it was the Mormons who settled there.

Bryce was like a different planet. We were greeted near the entrance by a large raven which landed on a fence near Dean and scrutinized him closely. Having gained his approval we continued on. There was magic in the air.

"[18]The meaning of the Raven symbol signifies that danger has passed and that good luck would follow. According to Native American legends and myths of some tribes the Raven played a part in their Creation myth. The raven escaped from the darkness of the cosmos and became the bringer of light to the world. The raven is associated with the creation myth because it brought light where there was only darkness. The raven is also believed to be a messenger of the spirit world. It is believed that ravens who fly high toward the heavens take prayers from the people to the spirit world and, in turn, bring back messages from the spiritual realm."

All around were towering rocks sculpted by the elements. They were known as 'Hoodoos' and they stretched for miles. It was like a vast audience listening and watching you as you walked. They morphed from pale peach to flame red in the burning sun.   With respect to Kenny's experience as a local trekker we obediently chose the Navajo Trail which led to the Peek-a-boo loop. The ochre landscape against the azure sky was stunning.   Yet despite the intense sun, pockets of bright, white snow clung to the base of the rocks.

I walked on ahead, keen for some solitude, whilst Dean took some photographs. I felt overcome with sadness, with so many questions in my head. Why did Alex have to die so young? How would I cope with this? What did I need to do? Is he with my mother? Is he okay? I asked the Indian ancestors for help with my grief, as I've always felt the Native Americans had a healthy attitude to death generally.

I sat on a bare tree trunk and sobbed from the bottom of my heart. There was no-one around so I could really let it out. Dean quietly appeared and whispered for me to look on my right. I turned and saw a beautiful bird hopping close to me. It had a black head and upper body with a fancy crest and its underbody and tail were an iridescent blue. He was cocking his head sideways looking at me. I was so surprised I stopped sobbing. It was a true encounter. He flew into a nearby tree to join a larger bird of the same family. For me in that moment I had no doubt it was a message from Alex telling me he was okay, he was with my Mam and that he would always be able to find me. It was deeply special, Dean was also struck by the antics of the bird. I thanked the ancestors, and just accepted that something important had occurred that really made me wonder. We discovered later the bird was called a Steller's Jay.

When the idea first came to me to plan a trip across America, the seed I planted was to seek out wonder, and help me recover from heartbreak and be reminded of how amazing the world is. I had long dreamt of exploring the US but I never really expected to. It does seem that people's lives go up and down, and the devastating lows can be matched by soaring highs if you allow yourself to leave your comfort zone and take a few risks. Reaching the Grand Canyon was at the heart of my pursuit of wonder. A friend once gave me a candle holder, which when lit illuminated the words "A wonderful life is a life full of wonder", and I believe this is very true.

So the Grand Canyon was the final National Park we'd chosen to visit. We found a motel nearby in Tusayan, Arizona, checked ourselves in, then proceeded towards the Southern Rim, where we would stay until sunset.

There are no words to describe the scale of the Canyon. The chasm is so vast we couldn't comprehend it. There isn't one cliff face, but more like 5 that descend down to the bottom. The Colorado River was a thin, silvery ribbon slithering across the valley floor like a snake on hot sand.

We were blessed with a clear sky; people started gathering, some with huge expensive looking cameras. I had brought my MP3 player and head phones so I could block everyone out and hear a few choice tracks by Dreadzone to accompany the sun's descent, "[21]Walk Tall" and

"[22]Just Let Go". Dean understood and enjoyed his own experience.

I like to buy a new perfume when I'm feeling particularly great so I can associate the aroma with the positive emotions and re-connect to them in the future. In the same way, I wanted to fuse the experience of the sunset to the music. A quiet descended over the area as we watched the sun dimming over the rocks. I was carried into the sky with the uplifting lyrics and far reaching melodies. As they played in my head, the sky became a blue tequila sunrise, with red and gold streaks condensing along the horizon. It was emotional, and despite my tears I felt really close to Alex and my Mam. I'd made it here and it was worth it. Slowly and gently the escarpment was cloaked in darkness. I had thrust my head through a false ceiling and my horizons were instantly broadened; I was ready to take a big step forward.

***

Miles above the Grand Canyon, Alex and Margaret were waiting excitedly with their guides, a large group of friends and some family members who had also passed over. They were gathered together for an important occasion. The Grand Canyon is a powerful energy centre, and at sunrise and sunset it is possible to link energetically with the people occupying the area, as the atmosphere is less dense at these times. The purpose of this particular gathering was to send transformative healing to individuals in a group meditation. People on earth would be drawn here for many reasons and, if open to receiving help, could experience significant emotional shifts.

Rose's brother and mother were excited as they anticipated an opportunity to connect with Rose on a deep level, when she visited at sunset with her partner Dean. Her desire to visit the canyon had sent an intention directly to them, which they had received as a flare of white light. Prayers were similarly acquired, but the information contained was different.

Rose could benefit greatly from the contact. Now she was more open to receiving healing than ever before. They both knew it would help her to keep moving forward through her grief, and there were many important developments coming her way that would bring her much more joy which they wanted to help her prepare for. However, it would take time for her heart to revitalize.

A single, beautiful note resonated around them and marked the beginning of the ceremony. The sky turned flame-red and birds shot across it like black darts. The veil between the worlds dissolved and it was possible to "see" everyone gathered around the canyon rim enjoying the sundown. The energy swirled around them as if a huge, invisible brush was mixing all the colours of the sunset together. Enchanting music accompanied the celestial spectacle. During the meditation, beams of intense light were focused on Rose's heart. The energy transmitted from Alex and Margaret to Rose was sublime, for them also.

They knew they had connected with Rose's soul, they recognized it. This intricately timed healing brought a powerful connection between them all.

***

The remainder of our time in America would be spent in Arizona. I'd read about Sedona and the special energy that existed, particularly around the red rock outcrops and crags.

We had a couple more days before catching our flight back from Phoenix, so needed to find some lodgings. We were both in a very positive place, and were riding on a wave of optimism and joy from the amazing places we had visited and the many people we had connected with. Americans like to hear your story as well as telling their own, and seemed genuinely interested in our travels and experiences.

The tourist office caught our eye on our way in to Sedona so we started there. An engaging young man with a funky haircut welcomed us inside and asked what we were looking for. On learning it was our last stop before home, he decided he wanted us to have a great memory to take home and offered us free accommodation at a holiday resort. The trade-off was a short tour the next day with a representative from the organisation. We were very happy with this, and it possibly ticked a box for him as he seemed just as elated. He also booked us into a much sought-after restaurant just before sunset and that was us sorted. I was starting to think that the energy in Sedona was a bit special.

The daily temperature was the hottest yet, so the free apartment, complete with large pool, was much appreciated. Sedona was laid back and really clean and attractive. There were crystal shops and alternative therapies for the mind, body and spirit. We enjoyed an evening stroll around the shops and bars after our evening meal.

On the final day we set off to climb Cathedral Rock. The colours of the landscape were again hot reds against a perfect blue sky, a dazzling combination. As we rounded the rock to head downwards, I happened upon a Navajo Indian lady who had spread a large shawl on the earth to display her handmade jewellery. This appealed to me far more than the shops, so I chose a necklace for myself which I was immediately attracted to. She explained that it was made from rock found at the Grand Canyon, and it would energise me, and this made it even more perfect. I also picked one for Charley, my friend back home, who was house sitting our Bonny cat.

Suffice to say the whole trip had been life changing and I knew I would return to America many times, However, I didn't relish returning home at all, going back to a job I didn't like, with people I didn't care for, who didn't care for me, and not being able to tell Alex about the trip that I had discussed with him when he was alive. I went back resolute that some important changes were going to be made and I wasn't putting up with trivia or people that pulled me down anymore.

The flight was really enjoyable but I

wanted it to last longer, I didn't want to go home, other than to see my precious cat Bonny, and neither did Dean.

On landing back in Newcastle, we collected our luggage off the carousel and walked out into the airport where people were waiting to collect passengers. Right in the middle of the small crowd was a man holding a large white sign that had ALEX written in large capital letters on it. It made me smile and shake my head in awe at the synchronicity; such a simple thing but quite literally a wonderful sign.

Birds of a Feather

Returning home and back to work in particular, was grim. The office was stiflingly boring. My previous role had ended, which I was okay about as 7 years is long enough to be promoting any initiative. I really wanted to leave, but my senior boss had coaxed me to try a different role in the department that needed someone like me to fill it. It was a new project that would help vulnerable people struggling to cope with anti-social behaviour. It didn't do a lot for me as I was working alongside a very ego driven woman; nevertheless, through taking on the role I came to realise that I needed to work directly with vulnerable people to give them the tools and support to put themselves back together. I became a volunteer for a local charity that helped victims of crime recover from the impact and get their lives back on track. I had made a promise to myself that in my 50th year I would leave the place I'd been working for the last 12 years whether I had a job to go to or not, so this was at least something I could do to occupy myself whilst I looked for paid work.

Heading home from work on the bus one day, I was overcome with emotion. I really missed Alex, and sometimes grief just hits you. "What is he doing and where is he?" I showed my ticket to the driver and hid my face as I grabbed the nearest free seat. I didn't want people to see me upset, so I kept my head down. The seat next to me was empty, but there was a man sitting opposite at right angles to me with a box next to him. I stared at the edge of the package where it was lit up by a shaft of sunlight, and read the words, 'Brother at your side' which was the company logo. I was quite shocked at first and couldn't believe what I was seeing, so I took a photograph to show Dean (see back cover). It was an answer to my question and a beautiful reminder that Alex wasn't too far away from me.

In September 2012 it would be Alex's 1st anniversary. I wanted to be abroad, so I booked a holiday to Cyprus for Dean and me. The weather was sensational. Coincidentally, we bumped into some old friends who were staying at the same hotel which was really nice, and we went on a few excursions with them as they'd hired a car.

In addition, Dean and I were keen to visit the Troodos Mountains and have a proper walk. I was feeling very sad that day and sometimes it's hard for couples to come together at these times. Deciding when and where to eat and reading maps can become a focus for discord; such trivial stuff is really just the tip of an emotional iceberg. Despite that, we managed to get ourselves on the appropriate bus to the start of a trail and begin our walk through the mountains.

The path was wide and littered with pine cones and a springy carpet of needles. Dean walked ahead. Both of us were still angry and keen to keep some distance from each other for the time being. I was feeling quite desolate and didn't know how to make myself feel better, and hoped the walk would change my state of mind. I noticed a bird sitting in a nearby tree. There weren't many signs of wildlife; perhaps the heat was keeping them hidden. It flew on ahead and eventually I caught up with Dean. The trail we chose took about six hours; it wound through the trees, then up along ochre-coloured, mountain passes that became quite narrow, and back down to woodland and larger paths. That little bird came with us the whole way. It would fly on ahead, and seemingly wait for us to catch up, then head off again and plot our journey. We both felt it was Alex once again sending confirmation he was around and bringing some real comfort to me at the time of his anniversary. It was an epic walk and we were cold at the end of it. At the start, we had sought shade in the trees, but moving into early evening we needed to put on every piece of clothing we'd brought. The little bird and the beautiful walk brought us right back into harmony. We were exhausted but exhilarated. I was now convinced that Alex made contact with me through encounters with birds.

"22Native American bird and animal symbols and totems are believed to represent the physical form of a spirit helper and guide. Bird symbols are very special to the Native Americans, their ability to soar above the clouds, perhaps to the heavens, and their sense of freedom inspired many. The many birds of North America feature as carved and painted totems with varying meanings to different tribes. However, because of their amazing power of flight, many are revered as bringers of messages

*and symbols of change. They include song birds,
water birds and birds of prey"*

A friend of mine is sure that her mother let
her know she was okay shortly after she died by
sending a Blue Tit that landed on her windowsill
and looked into her eyes, staying for an unusually
long length of time before flying off. I have no
doubt there are many more similar stories.

Back at our hotel, we showered then went
out for dinner and enjoyed a relaxing evening. The
next day was the anniversary of Alex's death, and I
wasn't sure how I would feel. Completing a whole
year without the person you've lost is a significant
milestone, but important dates and celebrations are
like crossing an emotional minefield; you just don't
know which one is going to blow up for you. It's a
disconcerting time.

Dean was fast asleep when I half woke up
and saw a man at the far end of our studio room. I
wondered what he was doing here, but didn't feel
frightened of him; he was medium height, fair
haired with a short sleeved top and trousers. I fell
back to sleep. When I woke again later, I
remembered the man and realised it was Alex I
had seen. It's strange how it didn't register at first,
but I know I wasn't properly awake. I was so
thrilled to have seen him, especially today.

The rest of our holiday consisted of
swimming, sunbathing, eating and relaxing. I'd
got through the first anniversary and knew I was
going to be okay. Every year I am either away on
holiday on Alex's anniversary, or doing something

I've never experienced before to celebrate his life, and I'm usually away for Maggie's birthday for the same reason.

***

On Thursday 20th December of the same year as the holiday to Cyprus, I visited the spiritual church near my home. I hadn't been often, but I still called in occasionally and hoped for some contact. As it happened I did get a message, and it was from a young medium called Jackie.

She opened with "Can anyone relate to the Mikado?" I recalled going to see the Mikado, a stage performance by Gilbert and Sullivan, with my Mam and sister when I was about 10 years old. We went to a few different productions, though I found them too long and boring. Anyway I put my hand up, along with a few other people.

"I'm being given freesias and the scent of them is important". Again I could relate to that, so I kept my hand up.

"I have a woman here who says someone understands the words Apple of my Eye", she continued. I thought of the birthday card my Mam had given me on my last birthday before she died. It had a beautiful drawing of a woman wearing a bonnet, plucking an apple from a tree and inside it said "You are the Apple of my Eye". I'd lost the card only a few years ago, and was really upset about this and still hold out the hope it will reappear. So it meant a lot to me. As it was, I was the only person to understand everything Jackie had said, so she drew nearer and focused on me.

A few days earlier, I had been really upset by some people I knew who had been hugely insensitive. Their thoughtlessness had hurt me deeply and I hadn't yet decided how to respond. Jackie made a reference to this, and told me she had a man wanting to say to me, "Don't let the bastards get you down!" This was something Alex had said to me when he was alive, so Jackie had my full attention now.

Jackie proceeded further, "I am being given a song which means a lot to you but it's also meant as advice for the situation; it's called "Walk Tall", I couldn't believe it, this was the Dreadzone track that had come to mean so much to me in relation to Alex. The moment she said it, I felt a surge of emotion inside me, then a split second later Jackie also felt it, as if I'd physically thrown something at her. She told me, half-heartedly to keep it as it was too much emotion for her. It was a short exchange but very powerful, and the emotions that crossed between me and Jackie were palpable. I thanked her so much for it and marvelled at the cleverness of the message to deliver so much in such a simple way.

When I got home that evening I recorded the night in great detail. I had decided that I wanted to write a book to express some of the exquisite power and beauty of the signs and messages I'd received in my life. They had brought me so much comfort and strength and had helped me to overcome the loss of people I thought I couldn't live without. These experiences also gave me the courage to be more authentic in my relationships, and hammered home the understanding that life really is precious, and for some it is very short.

Sometimes I would imagine what Alex and my Mam got up to in their "new" life; what they did for work, if anything, and whether they thought I was doing okay? I so look forward to seeing them again when its my turn to leave Earth, but in the meantime I'd like to think they aren't too far from my side.

Starman

I hadn't written anything towards this book for over a year, then something happened on my 50th birthday that I had to write about. I was in a luxury hotel room for my birthday when it was announced on the large TV that David Bowie had died. I felt a blow to my body and couldn't take it in.

The previous night had been a truly magical night, a meal with special friends in a private dining room at a hotel. I was at least spared from hearing about it until the Next Day. The world went into mourning; I was amazed by the reaction to his death, I mean *I* knew he was extremely special, unique and immensely inspiring, as did millions of other fans, but I didn't think he would get the recognition from the world media that he actually deserved. News of his death was everywhere. Every channel, radio station, social media went berserk, and celebrities were falling over themselves to associate themselves with him, either through their own emotional tributes or through referencing a time when they met or worked with him, however brief. Tributes from member's of Bowie's inner circle, namely Brian Eno, Tony Visconti and Gary Oldman, offered much needed comfort and reassurance around David Bowie's mysteriously private and sudden exit from our world. Very few people outside of his family knew of his 18 month battle with cancer, and that is the way he wanted it. He continued to create music right up until his death.

It is rare not to have an inkling of a celebrity's demise given the supersonic transfer of information around the globe, combined with the public's obsession for gossip. Yet he ensured his privacy and achieved a truly dignified departure like nothing we have seen before.

Whether you loved him or hated him, what became apparent to people of all ages was that his music had been the background to their lives, and as a consequence the replaying of his vast catalogue, following his death, evoked personal memories and transported people back to their younger selves.

[23]His first UK hit was in 1969 with the release of the single Space Oddity, and he achieved chart topping success right up until his death and beyond, as his final album, Black Star, took the number one spot in many countries in the wake of his death. It became Bowie's first and only album to reach number one on the Billboard 200 album chart in the U.S. The album remained at the number one position in the UK charts for three weeks, before being replaced by one of Bowie's compilation albums, Best of Bowie. Numerous albums from his back catalogue shot into the top 40, including Hunky Dory, The Rise and Fall of Ziggy Stardust, Aladdin Sane, Low, Let's Dance, Nothing has Changed and Next Day. Very few artists have had such a long and successful music career (47 years since Space Oddity was released).

As a diehard fan, having a new album to absorb and cherish following his death was a real treasure comfort. He was doing his thing right up until the end. It engenders a sense of life after death, especially if further material is released in the future. It's an incredible parting gift. He inspired us through his pure creative expression and portrayal of otherworldliness, and has now returned to his celestial home having fulfilled his contract here on Earth.

I actually had a premonition of his death. Following the release of his Next Day album in 2013 I studied the image of him inside CD and "knew" that he wasn't well and thought I could see the ravaging effect of cancer in his face. However there were no reports at all. On January 10th, the day of his death, I was getting ready, preparing to head down to the hotel for my 50th birthday meal. I was packing my overnight case and felt compelled to dig out a Bowie T shirt to sleep in which I hadn't worn for many months. I had been feeling very anxious during the build-up to my birthday, and spoke to Dean about how I suddenly felt an awful sense of loss, as if I had just lost a friend, and it made me sob.

As Dean got ready upstairs, I went outside and stood on the decking in the garden and looked up to see a beautiful section of orange and red sky. I stared at it for about 10-15 minutes and felt that it reminded me that when we lose people, life goes on at another level, and deep down I know this. Since my near drowning in France, the sky has always been an incredible source of comfort for me, it holds the secrets of the Universe and imparts knowledge if you allow yourself to drift up and into it. All of a sudden, I felt completely different, as if something had left me. I felt calm and joyful and headed back inside, looking forward to my night with no further anxiety. I wanted to take my David Bowie compilation to play during the meal as I thought it would be more accessible to the motley crew I'd invited, but I had lent it to someone. It was a magical evening, and afterwards in our hotel room I opened my presents from Dean which included David Bowie's new album "Black Star" and a brand new illustrated biography of David Bowie, spanning his life. I was over the moon with them, but despite being tired and a bit worse for wear from drinking, I remember opening the book and feeling a sense of gloom and thinking this will be very sad to view after he dies, which, as it was already after midnight and we were now into Monday 11th January 2016, he already had.

I think we all receive so much more information emotionally than we realise, if we let ourselves. The mind is an amazing antenna. I have no doubt I was picking something up, and find some comfort in the fact, as it made me feel connected to him. It also felt appropriate that the news broke of his death on one of my milestone birthdays. Fifty is an interesting age, there is still so much that can be achieved, though it is also definitely nearer to the end of a person's life than the beginning. I felt inspired yet again by David Bowie and his unrelenting creativity and sheer productiveness, despite many setbacks and challenges that he had to deal with in his personal life and career. I wanted to get on with fulfilling what I came here to achieve.

For my 50th year I had decided an important trip was in order, and America was probably in the mix. A few weeks after my birthday, in a moment of inspiration, I knew what I wanted to do. I was going to visit the three homes that were most significant in David Bowie's life; 40, Stanfield Road, Brixton, 155, Haupstrasse, Schoneberg, Berlin and 285, Lafayette Street, New York, and that is what I did, with Dean. At his current home in New York I left a card with a friendly, glamorous receptionist who promised me she would pass it on to David Bowie's wife and daughter, which I hope she did.

"Better by far you should forget and smile than that you should remember and be sad"
Christina Rossetti

Of course it is even better if you can remember ***and*** smile...............

Recipes from my mother's cookbook;

Banana Fritters

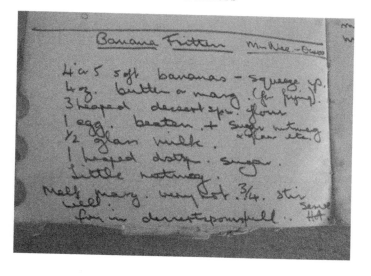

4 or 5 soft bananas - squeeze up
4 oz butter or marg (for frying)
3 heaped dessertspoons of flour
1 egg beaten add sugar nutmeg, flour etc
1/2 glass of milk
1 heaped dessertspoon of sugar
a little nutmeg
Melt marg very hot
fry in dessertspoonfuls
Serve hot.

Cheese Scones

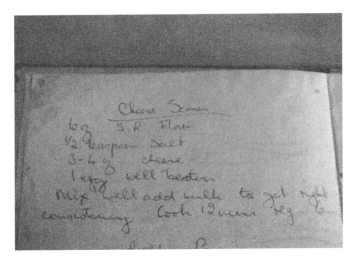

6 oz self raising flour
1/2 teaspoon salt
3-4 oz cheese (keep some for the tops)
1 egg well beaten
Mix well, add milk to get right consistency,
sprinkle some cheese on the top.
Cook for 12 minutes Gas mark 6

Kunzle Cake

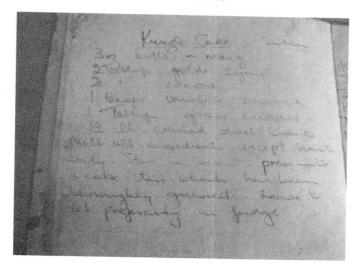

3 oz butter or marg
2 tablespoons golden syrup
2 tablespoons cocoa
1 teaspoon vanilla essence
1/2 lb crushed digestive biscuits
Melt all ingredients except biscuits. Slowly stir in
biscuits. Press into a cake tin which has been
thoroughly greased. Leave to set preferably in the
fridge.

Lemon Curd

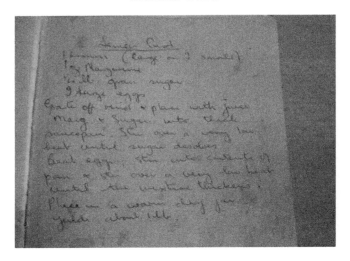

1 lemon (large or 2 small)
1 oz margarine
1/4 lb granulated sugar
2 large eggs
Grate off rind and place with juice, marg and sugar into thick saucepan. Stir over a very low heat until sugar dissolves.
Beat eggs stir into contents of pan and stir over a very low heat until the mixture thickens.
Place in a warm dry jar.
Yields about 1 lb.

References

1   Goodreads.com. 2020. *A Quote By Elisabeth Kübler-Ross*. [online] Available at: <https://www.goodreads.com/quotes/202404-the-most-beautiful-people-we-have-known-are-those-who> [Accessed 14 June 2020].

2   Goodreads.com. 2020. *A Quote By Vine Deloria Jr.*. [online] Available at: <https://www.goodreads.com/quotes/160879-religion-is-for-people-who-re-afraid-of-going-to-hell> [Accessed 14 June 2020].

3   En.wikipedia.org. 2020. *The Shire*. [online] Available at: <https://en.wikipedia.org/wiki/Shire_(Middle-earth)> [Accessed 14 June 2020].

4   David Bowie. 2020. *Aladdin Sane — David Bowie*. [online] Available at: <https://www.davidbowie.com/aladdin-sane> [Accessed 14 June 2020].

5   En.wikipedia.org. 2020. *Tom Brown's School Days*. [online] Available at:<https://en.wikipedia.org/wiki/Tom_Brown%27s_Schooldays> [Accessed 14 June 2020].

6   Bodenner, C., 2020. *Track Of The Day: 'Heroes' By David Bowie*. [online] The Atlantic. Available at: <https://www.theatlantic.com/notes/2016/10/track-of-the-day-heroes-by-david-bowie/505382/> [Accessed 14 June 2020].

7   Business Insider. 2020. *GERMANY: Thank You David Bowie For Helping Bring Down The Berlin Wall*. [online] Available at: <https://www.businessinsider.com/germany-thanks-david-bowie-for-helping-bring-down-berlin-wall-2016-1> [Accessed 14 June 2020].

8   En.wikipedia.org. 2020. *19 (Song)*. [online] Available at: <https://en.wikipedia.org/wiki/19_(song)> [Accessed 14 June 2020].

9   IMDb. 2020. *Mr Benn (TV Mini-Series 1971–2005) - Imdb*. [online] Available at:
<https://www.imdb.com/title/tt0065322/>
[Accessed 14 June 2020].

10   En.wikipedia.org. 2020. *In Rainbows*. [online] Available at: <https://en.wikipedia.org/wiki/In_Rainbows> [Accessed 14 June 2020].

11   En.wikipedia.org. 2020. *Dreadzone*. [online] Available at: <https://en.wikipedia.org/wiki/Dreadzone> [Accessed 14 June 2020].

12   Deathcafe.com. 2020. *Welcome To Death Cafe*. [online] Available at: <http://deathcafe.com/> [Accessed 14 June 2020].

13   En.wikipedia.org. 2020. *Here Comes The Sun*. [online] Available at:
<https://en.wikipedia.org/wiki/Here_Comes_the_Sun>
[Accessed 14 June 2020].

14   Dreadzone.com. 2020. *Changes – Dreadzone*. [online] Available at:
<https://www.dreadzone.com/music/eye-on-the-horizon/track/changes/>
[Accessed 14 June 2020].

15   En.wikipedia.org. 2020. *Basil King*. [online] Available at: <https://en.wikipedia.org/wiki/Basil_King> [Accessed 14 June 2020].

16   IMDb. 2020. *Starsky And Hutch (TV Series 1975–1979) - Imdb*. [online] Available at:
<https://www.imdb.com/title/tt0072567/>
[Accessed 14 June 2020].

17   En.wikipedia.org. 2020. *Twinkie*. [online] Available at: <https://en.wikipedia.org/wiki/Twinkie>
[Accessed 14 June 2020].

18   IMDb. 2020. *Bill & Ted's Excellent Adventure (1989) - Imdb*. [online] Available at:
<https://www.imdb.com/title/tt0096928/>
[Accessed 14 June 2020].

19   https://www.warpaths2peacepipes.com

20   Dreadzone.com. 2020. *Walk Tall – Dreadzone*. [online] Available at:
<https://www.dreadzone.com/music/eye-on-the-

horizon/track/walk-tall/>
[Accessed 14 June 2020].

21   Dreadzone.com. 2020. *Just Let Go – Dreadzone*.
[online] Available at:
<https://www.dreadzone.com/music/eye-on-the-
horizon/track/just-let-go/>
[Accessed 14 June 2020].

22   https://www.warpaths2peacepipes.com

23   En.wikipedia.org. 2020. *David Bowie*. [online]
Available at: <https://en.wikipedia.org/wiki/David_Bowie>
[Accessed 14 June 2020].

I have tried to recreate events, locales and conversations from my memories of them. In order to maintain their anonymity in some instances I have changed the names of individuals and places, I may have changed some identifying characteristics and details such as physical properties, occupations and places of residence.

Printed in Great Britain
by Amazon